DANNY ORLIS
AND THE
DRUGSTORE MYSTERY

DANNY ORLIS
AND THE
DRUGSTORE MYSTERY

BERNARD PALMER

Danny Orlis and the Drugstore Mystery
© 2024 by Bernard Palmer
All rights reserved. First edition 1962.
Second edition 2024.

Cover image: Adobe Firefly
Character illustrations: John Ball
Editor: Jon D. Fogdall

Aneko Press Youth

www.anekopress.com

Aneko Press, Life Sentence Publishing, and our logos are trademarks of Life Sentence Publishing, Inc.
203 E. Birch Street
P.O. Box 652
Abbotsford, WI 54405

JUVENILE FICTION / Religious / Christian / Action & Adventure

Paperback ISBN: 979-8-88936-004-9
eBook ISBN: 979-8-88936-005-6
10 9 8 7 6 5 4 3 2 1
Available where books are sold

CONTENTS

CHAPTER 1

"AN UNWELCOME INVITATION"

Hal Seybold left the house at the usual time and hurried toward school, his back hunched against the harsh winter wind. He was not particularly tall for his age, but was squarely built, with a jaw that jutted forward very much like his dad's, Big Ed Seybold.

He had covered half the distance to school when Doug Ellis caught up with him. "Hi," Doug sang out. "What's new?"

Hal glanced at him. "Not much."

They walked on for half a block or more without speaking. Hal scuffed his boots in the new snow and kicked a bit of ice along the walk ahead of him.

"Where were you yesterday?" Doug continued after a time. "We stopped over your way in the afternoon, but you weren't home."

Hal hesitated. "Dad and I were over at Danny and Kay's for dinner. We didn't get back until three o'clock or so."

Doug Ellis laughed almost sneeringly. "I'll bet I can tell you what Danny was doing, too. He was probably trying to preach to your old man, wasn't he?"

Hal colored, but he did not speak.

"I never knew Danny or that wife of his to have anybody over there that they didn't try to preach to before he got away. That's what he tried with me, but it didn't work, I can tell you that. I'm too smart to get hooked on that religion they always try to peddle."

"They just invited us over for dinner," Hal told him. "That's all."

"Sure. Sure. They just invited you over to dinner." He laughed knowingly. "Now don't try to give me that stuff. I know better."

The Seybold boy did not argue with him. Another short space of silence followed.

"Sure wish you had been home yesterday," Doug went on. "I was going to take you to the show with me. You sure missed a good one."

"As far as I'm concerned," Hal told him, "I'm going to miss them all."

Doug grinned. "You'll get over that in time, when you see that you're missing out on all the fun."

They crossed the street and went up the school steps.

"We did go to the show yesterday afternoon," Doug continued, "but what I really came over to your place for was to introduce you to a couple of new guys who just moved to town. You'd really like them."

"New guys?"

"Yeah, new guys. They just moved to town Saturday, and their dad will be working at the mine the same as everyone else. You'd really go for them, Hal. They're great."

They stopped at their lockers and slipped out of their coats.

"Are they in our grade?"

"One of them is. The other is a year or two behind us. But he's a great kid. I tell you, he's not scared of anything."

At the door to their home room Doug paused. "Hang around awhile after school tonight and walk home with us," he said. "You've just got to meet them."

Hal nodded reluctantly. He caught a glimpse of the new guys in the corridors during the day, but it was not until after school that he was introduced to them. He waited just inside the main door until Doug came with the two boys.

"This is Pete Nolan, Hal," he said, "and this is his younger brother, Vic."

"Hi." Hal Seybold stuck out his hand.

The boys left the schoolhouse together and Doug turned to the newcomers. "This is the guy I've been telling you about," he said. "Course, he's a little gone on religion right now, but outside of that he's really all right."

Pete Nolan, the older brother, grinned. "That might even help us a little," he said, "if someone is gettin' on to us. We had a preacher's kid in our gang back in the town where we used to live. Everybody thought he wouldn't do a thing." He laughed shortly. "But that guy could break more windows in 10 minutes than any of the rest of us."

Hal stared at them. "What are you guys talking about?" he asked. "What are you planning to do?"

Doug's smile flashed. "What'd I tell you, Pete? I knew Hal would be right along with us. Go on, tell him how much fun you used to have before you moved here."

Both Pete and his younger brother, Vic, were grinning broadly. "Should I tell him about the time we slashed the tires on the principal's car or the time we messed up the chemistry lab at the new high school?" Pete asked.

"I don't think I care to hear about either one," Hal answered.

The smiles faded. "What's the matter?" Pete demanded, a surly scowl clouding his young face. "Are you too good for us?"

"I just don't go for stuff like that, that's all."

Pete Nolan turned to Doug accusingly. "I thought you said Hal would be throwing in with us.

"Just give him time," Doug said lamely. "He'll come in, all right."

"He'd better," Pete muttered darkly. "That's all I can say." If he doesn't, it'll ruin everything." His dark eyes narrowed ominously, and he took a step or two toward Hal. "How about it, Seybold?" he asked threateningly. "Are you going to join us or not?"

Hal moved back half a step, eyeing the bigger guy warily, the way he eyed his dad when Big Ed was mad and apt to hit him with or without cause.

"Don't stand there all day!" Pete snarled. "Are you throwing in with us or not? Answer me!"

Doug Ellis was quick to break in. "I've already told you he'll join our gang, Pete," he said. "If I hadn't thought that, I wouldn't have had you say a word to him about it. Hal's the best friend I've got, and he's a regular guy. Just don't crowd him. Give him a little time and he'll come around. I'll vouch for him!"

The older Nolan boy relaxed slightly, and a twisted smile came to play furtively on his lips. "Okay," he said impatiently. "Okay, if you say so. But I don't like this stalling. I want a guy to speak up when I talk to him. I want him to know I'm the boss."

The muscles in Hal Seybold's throat tightened and his breathing was fast and hard. A guy like Pete Nolan would just as soon hit a guy as look at him. And he was big!

Vic turned to Hal. "You're in luck and don't know it, Hal," he said. "We wouldn't take you into our gang no matter what you said or did if it weren't for Doug, here. We're careful about who we let in, aren't we, Pete?"

"We've got to be," Pete retorted. "We can't have some guy lipping off to everyone about what we do." He turned to Doug as though Hal wasn't even there. "That's another thing," he said. "Before we take anyone in as a member, we're all going to vote on him. And if he gets even one vote against him, he doesn't get in." That's final."

Vic nodded his complete agreement. "And if anybody squeals on us, it's going to be too bad for him." He lowered his voice. "The fact is," he went on, "it's going to be too bad for *anybody* who tells anything on us or does anything to anyone of us. We're going to stick together."

Doug Ellis laughed at that, nervously. "Sounds all right to me," he said. "It sounds great."

There was a short silence. The three of them were tensely watching Hal – watching and waiting for his answer. He swallowed hard, and a dry, hacking cough escaped his lips. He knew what they were thinking as surely as though they were shouting it. The breath squeezed out of his lungs.

Pete Nolan made the first move. "Well," he demanded harshly, "how about it? Are you going to be one of our charter members, or aren't you?"

Hal bit his lower lip to keep it from trembling. "I–I don't think so," he stammered.

The tension grew. Anger flashed in Pete's eyes, and when he spoke his voice was harsh and belligerent. "What do you mean?" he exclaimed. "What do you mean, you don't think so?"

Hal stood his ground. "I'm not interested in joining a gang like you guys are talking about. And you shouldn't be interested in it either, Doug. It sounds to me as though it's a good way of getting into some real trouble."

Pete spit contemptuously at Hal's feet, but when he spoke, he addressed Doug. "I thought you said he was all right, Ellis." There was accusation in his voice. "I thought you said he'd go along with us, and that all we had to do was to ask him."

Color seeped up into Doug's cheeks. "Don't get so shook up, Nolan," he said defensively. "Give him time. He'll be all right. He's just a little slow to make up his mind, that's all."

"Well," Pete snorted, "he'd better come around. That's all I can say. He'd better!" Deliberately he moved toward Hal, fists clenched and his face now dark with anger. "There's a thing or two you'd just as well get straight," he threatened. "If I ask a guy to come into my gang, he comes in! He comes in or else!"

Hal's gaze met Pete's and held there. A silent prayer for help and courage went up from his heart. He was trembling inside, but when he spoke his voice was calm and clear.

"It isn't going to happen this time, Pete. I'm not interested in doing the kind of things you've been talking about. And you shouldn't be, either. You guys'll get into a real jam if you start anything like that. And it won't take long."

Pete laughed sarcastically. "I see what's wrong with you now. You're chicken! You're too scared to join our club."

"I wouldn't want to destroy property and do things like that," Hal said, "because I'm a Christian; also, it's against the law."

Doug Ellis broke in quickly. "Now listen, Hal," he said, "don't get so worked up about this. Pete was just telling us some of the things he, Vic and some of the guys where they used to live did, and how much fun they had. That doesn't mean we'll have to do the same things. It's going to be a club. We'll all have a say in what we do, won't we, Pete?"

The older Nolan boy grinned. "Sure we will," he said. "And besides, you don't need to worry that we're going to get into trouble with the law. Back home we were hauled down to the police station and questioned a couple of times, but they weren't able to pin a thing on us. Not a single thing, so there's no sweat there."

Vic touched Hal on the arm. "I was scared at first, too, Hal. But those cops weren't able to get anything on us. We were too slick for them." He took a deep breath. "And another thing," he said, "if you're a member of the club and anyone bothers you – anyone at all, all you've got to do is tell the rest of us and we'll take care of him – but good!"

Hal was slow in speaking. The Nolan brothers pressed close to him; their eyes ablaze. "That doesn't interest me, Vic," Hal said. "I've never had any trouble before, and I don't think I'll have any now."

Pete pushed against him, forcing him to back away. "Don't be too sure," he warned. "If you don't come into our club, just don't be too sure that you won't have any trouble!" He exhaled slowly, hate creasing his young face. "I'm going to be good to you,

Seybold," he rasped, "because you're a good friend of Doug's. I'm going to let you off with a warning. If you talk to anyone about this – anyone at all – while you're deciding to come in with us, it's going to be too bad for you! Understand?" He grasped Doug by the arm and pivoted suddenly. "Come on, we can't waste any more time on him!"

With that the three of them strode away.

Hal remained motionless while they turned the corner and disappeared from view. He took off his heavy mitten and wiped the perspiration from under the rim of his fur-lined cap with a shaking hand. Although he hadn't noticed it before, the cold seemed to have increased a dozen fold until it drove to the very depths of his being. He crossed the street hurriedly.

A moment or two later Jim Morgan called out to him. "Hey, Hal! Wait up!"

Hal stopped and turned to wait for his friend. Jim looked at him incredulously. "What's wrong with you, Hal?" he asked curiously.

"Why?"

"You look as though you saw a ghost or something."

Hal shuddered. "Maybe I did."

Then, before Jim could ask him anything more, he changed the subject quickly. He wanted to tell Jim about Pete and Vic Nolan and the club Doug was helping them organize. He wanted to ask him to pray for him and for them. But he didn't dare. Not when Pete Nolan was the kind of a guy he was!

CHAPTER 2

A WARNING

The next day Hal Seybold met Doug Ellis on the way to school. He expected Doug to talk to him about joining the gang with him and the Nolan brothers; however, Doug did not mention it immediately.

"Did you remember about that English test we're supposed to have this morning?" Hal asked.

Doug laughed. "That's the least of my worries," he said airily. "I'm not concerned about getting a good grade in this English test."

There was a strange tone in his voice. Hal noticed it and glanced at him. "Don't tell me that you've started studying in English, Doug."

He chuckled. "Nothing like that." Then he looked about to see that no one was close and lowered his voice. "I promised Pete Nolan that I wouldn't say anything to anyone about it," he murmured guardedly, "but since you've been invited into the gang,

I think it would be all right to let you in on it." He paused, eyes glinting brightly with excitement.

Hal broke in quickly. "I haven't promised to go into the gang, Doug," he said, "and I don't intend to. I just want you to remember that."

"No, but you will!" Doug said confidently. "Wait until you hear what we've got lined up. And wait 'til I tell you what we've done. You'll be begging to join." He lowered his voice to a thin taut whisper. "Pete found out that we were going to have this mimeographed true-false test, see? So he slipped in and snitched a copy of it when nobody was looking." A triumphant grin twisted Doug's face. "Their copy even has the answers on it," he continued. "So I've got the questions and the answers. All of them. This is one test when I don't have to worry about getting a good grade."

Concern flashed across Hal's face and kindled twin flames in his eyes. "You shouldn't have done that, Doug," he retorted. "It isn't honest."

His companion snorted his derision. "Who's going to find out about it? Answer me that."

"Whether you get caught or not doesn't have anything to do with whether it's honest, Doug," Hal said. "But sooner or later you will get caught. And then it'll be too bad for you and everyone else who has been cheating."

Doug Ellis drew himself up proudly. "What's the matter, Hal? Are you jealous?"

"I should say not." He spoke firmly.

"You could use an A in English as well as I can. You aren't doing so hot in the grade department that you couldn't stand a little help."

"Maybe not," Hal said, "but if I get an A, I'm going to earn it."

Doug leaned over and almost whispered in his ear. "You won't have to worry about anyone finding out," he continued. "I'll slip you the questions and answers too. The teacher'll never know the difference."

Hal shook his head. "I mean it, Doug, I'm not interested at all. I don't want to have anything to do with that test paper."

Fear flickered momentarily in Doug's eyes. "You tell on me, Hal Seybold, and you'll wish you hadn't!" He stopped and took hold of his companion's arm. "Now you've got to join our gang!"

Hal jerked away from Doug and stepped back. For a brief instant, the boys glared at one another. Anger still clouded Doug's eyes and twisted his mouth. His fists knotted threateningly.

"You've got to join our gang now!" he cried.

"I've already told you that I'm not going to."

Doug snorted. "Wait 'til I tell Pete Nolan," he blustered. "We'll see whether you'll join or not. We'll make you!"

Hal stood his ground. "I don't have to do anything I don't want to do," he said, "and I sure wouldn't join that gang of yours."

Doug forced the scowl away with a smile. "You just think you wouldn't like to get in our gang," he coaxed. "We've already had a lot of fun. More fun than I ever had in my life before. Why, if you'd just come into our gang for a little while – a couple of weeks even – I'll bet you never would want to drop out."

Hal shook his head. "I know enough about it already to know that the things you're planning aren't what a Christian should do. It's just no place for me."

Doug drew himself up defensively. "You don't need to think you're so much. We're just as good as you are."

The Seybold boy did not answer him.

"And if you don't come into our gang, you'll really be in a jam!" he warned. "Just wait until I tell Pete! You know how tough he is! You know what he'll do to you!"

Hal Seybold's breath exploded from his lungs and his mouth went hot and dry. Pete Nolan was four inches taller than he was and outweighed him by thirty pounds. But it was neither his size nor weight that turned the young Christian's blood to ice. It was that tough droop to Pete's mouth that Doug was already copying, and the hard glint in his eyes.

"I still don't intend to go into your gang," Hal said quietly. He spoke with a firmness that surprised himself. "And if you know what's best for you, Doug, you won't have anything to do with it, either. It's bad medicine."

With that Hal pivoted and started for the school. Doug ran and caught up with him. "You–you aren't going to say anything to the teacher about what I told you of that English test, are you?" His voice was pleading.

Hal hesitated.

"I–I was really just kidding about that test," he said, "Pete didn't steal it." He spoke rapidly, trying to convince Hal of the truth of his words. "We–we were just talking about taking it. Saying how easy it would be if–if we wanted to. We don't have the test and answers. Honest, we don't."

Hal studied his face carefully. "If you have those test answers, Doug," he warned, "you'd better not use them. You'll get caught and get yourself into a lot of trouble."

Doug took hold of Hal's arm again, pleadingly. "Promise me you won't tell the teacher what I've just told you. There isn't any truth in it. It would just make you a liar."

"I'm not going to run to the teacher with the story," Hal told him, "but if she should ask me I–I'll have to tell her the truth. I want you to know that."

The Ellis boy's temper flared. "That's just about like you!" he cried. "Well, I'm going to tell you this much! If she finds out we'll know who told her, and we'll know who to come looking for! So just you watch your step, Hal Seybold! That's all I can tell you!"

Hal's heart pounded fiercely, but he did not back away. "Talking isn't going to change my mind. I can tell you that much, Doug Ellis."

His friend scowled bitterly and strode away, leaving him standing there. And when Hal met him in the hall later in the morning, Doug would not speak to him. He must have talked to Pete and Vic Nolan, too, for they gave him that same threatening stare.

In spite of himself Hal felt his pulse quicken and the color leave his cheeks.

In English class that morning the teacher called the students to attention. "As you know," she began evenly, "we are having a quiz this morning."

Hal glanced in Pete Nolan's direction just in time to see a knowing wink pass between him and Doug. A brief, wordless prayer went up from his heart, a prayer for his pal Doug and the other two brothers.

The teacher moved to the side of her desk and paused for a moment or two, drawing the class to attention by her very manner. "I had planned on giving a true-false quiz this morning," she went on. "However, when I went to get the mimeographed quiz a few minutes ago, I discovered the master sheet with both the questions and answers was missing."

A gasp went up from the classroom.

The teacher looked about the room slowly, her eyes resting briefly on one and then another. "It was very disappointing to me to think that anyone in this room would actually steal a quiz and the answers." She walked behind her desk to the other side of the room. "Rather than take a chance on having someone in here who would have an unfair advantage over the rest of you, I am going to give another test that I have prepared."

Doug's face became slightly paler.

"The fact that we are not using the stolen quiz does not lessen the seriousness of what has been done," she concluded. "I am sure Mr. Garber will go into the matter very thoroughly, so the guilty party or parties may be punished."

Doug turned in his seat and glared hard at Hal. When the class was over, he caught him in the hall. "What did you do?" he demanded. "Squeal on us?"

He shook his head. "If I did, she would have called you guys into Mr. Garber's office. You should know that."

Doug was startled as Hal spoke aloud and quickly looked around to be sure no one was within hearing distance. "Watch what you're saying!" he whispered. "If somebody hears you, we really will be in a jam."

CHAPTER 3

A PROMISE MADE

Hal had been so concerned about his father and the problems in his own spiritual life the next few days that he had all but forgotten Pete Nolan and Doug Ellis. He forgot them, that is, until they stopped him one morning on the way to school.

He managed a weak little grin. "Hi, fellas."

They acted as though they had not even heard his greeting. They stood in front of him, blocking his path. Pete pushed close to him and looked down into his eyes. "Well, Seybold," he asked dryly, "what's your answer?"

Hal's lips began to tremble, and it was a moment or two before he could talk. "W-what do you mean?" he stammered.

"Did you hear that, Ellis? He sounds like a wise guy!" He stepped close to Hal and took hold of his coat menacingly. "You know what we mean! Are you going to join our gang, or aren't you?"

There was a brief, painful silence. Hal tried to back away, but Pete tightened the grip on his coat and hauled him close with a powerful arm. "When I talk to you, answer me! Are you going to join up with us or not?"

Hal's lips parted and a hot flush surged over him.

Doug blustered close, mimicking the bigger boy's every motion. "Answer, Pete," he put in, "or we'll both let you have it! Are you going to join our gang, or are you too chicken?"

Hal swallowed hard, but he spoke bravely. "I've already told you, Doug. I'm a Christian. I can't join your gang."

With a quick movement Pete loosened his grip on Hal's coat and grabbed his arm, twisting it savagely. Hal almost cried out with pain. "You'd better change your mind, Seybold," Pete warned, "We're not takin' this kind of talk from you for very long! Just get that into your head!"

Doug glanced about to see that no one was watching them. "You squealed on us at school," he said, "We're not giving you a chance to do it again. You've got to join up with us whether you want to or not."

"That's right, Seybold! We're giving you one more chance. Either you throw in with us, or it's going to be too bad for you! Get me?"

Hal wrenched free from Pete and retreated a step or two, rubbing his arm gingerly.

Pete laughed. "Hurts a little, doesn't it?" he demanded. "That's just a sample of what you'll get if you don't throw in with us, Seybold! Just a sample." He made a quick, menacing gesture as though he was going to grab Hal's arm again. His laughter was hoarse and taunting as Hal ducked to escape him.

"We're going to be good to you, Hal," he went on. "Real good! We'll give you another week to make up your mind."

"But I already know what I'm going to do," Hal retorted. Though his heart was pounding furiously, his voice was firm and strong.

A strange, surprised look came to Pete Nolan's eyes, a look almost like fear. "You'd better take my advice and take the whole week to think it over!" he snarled. Taking a step or two closer to Hal, he lowered his voice. "And if you know what's good for you, you won't say anything to anyone about this. Understand?"

He started away, but Doug Ellis hung back.

"Are you going to let him off that easy, Pete?" he asked, his voice hostile.

"He'll find out how easy I am on him if he doesn't join up," he replied. "Come on. We've got things to do!"

Hal stared after them. His breath came in thin, wavering gasps.

Although he continued to pray regularly, he could see no real change in his father. Big Ed watched everything he did and took every opportunity to be abusive, even more, it seemed, than ever before. The evening ritual became the same. When his father came home from work, he looked around critically.

"Why ain't you got those dishes done?" he demanded.

Hal glanced at him in surprise. "But, dad," Hal protested, "you told me that you wanted me to clean the house and make the beds right after school. So that's what I started on."

Big Ed glowered at him. "I told you to do them dishes, too. Do you think I want to wait half the night for my supper after workin' down in the mine all day?" His voice raised. "You're gettin' to be the most insulting, sassy kid I ever saw, and you're lazier every day. I'm tellin' you this much. I ain't workin' down in that mine for eight hours and then comin' home to do dishes. And I ain't aimin' to eat on dirty plates, neither! Now get in there and get them dishes done b'fore I whop you!"

Hal did as he was told, without comment.

"And when you get that done," he snarled, "get in there and finish makin' them beds!"

Color leaped to Hal's cheeks and his temples pounded furiously. He felt hot tears in his eyes. But, in spite of the anger that surged within him, he forced a smile to his lips. "O.K., Dad," he said, "I'll fix the beds just as soon as I get the dishes done!"

Big Ed scowled unresponsively. "Don't you get smart with me or I'll let you have a good one on the side of the head! I'm not takin' no lip off a smart-aleck kid. I'll let you know that much right now!"

He threw himself into his chair and sat reading his newspaper until Hal had finished supper.

* * *

Over at the Orlis home, Jim Morgan made a suggestion at their family devotions that night. "We should have prayer for Hal," he said, "His dad's sure been giving him a rough time lately. The poor guy can't do anything to suit him."

Danny Orlis nodded. "Hal mentioned it to me in church Sunday. It sounded as though he is having trouble."

That evening after devotions, Danny and Kay went into their bedroom together. "Danny, I feel so sorry for Hal," she said. "I know just what he's going through."

"So do I. But maybe God is teaching him the lesson of patience and self-control."

"But it's so hard to understand why and how God works at times."

* * *

Hal avoided Pete Nolan and Doug Ellis for a day or two after the week was up. But the time came when he could no longer dodge them. They caught him on his way to the grocery store on Saturday morning.

Pete blustered up to him. "Doug and me have been lookin' all over for you, Seybold!" he began severely. "Where've you been?"

"I've been around."

Doug pushed close to him. "How about it?" he asked boldly. "Are you going to join our gang, or aren't you?"

Hal's whole being trembled. "I–I already told you a dozen times," he said. "I can't join your gang, even if I wanted to."

"Who's to stop you, Seybold?" he demanded. "That's what I'd like to know!"

"You can keep it a secret, Hal," Doug said. "We're not tellin' everybody our business. We won't let anyone know that you're in the gang."

Hal turned toward him. "That's not what I'm talking about."

Doug's eyes narrowed and his young face grew dark with anger. "We're givin' you one last chance!"

Pete and Doug both glared at him with hostile eyes.

"We shouldn't be doin' this, Seybold," Pete grated. "We already told you what was going to happen if you turned us down again. But we like you. We don't want to cause you any more trouble. So you've got just exactly forty-eight hours to make up your mind to come in with us. Forty-eight hours."

The Ellis boy stepped up to Hal and spoke with authority. "And if you don't, Hal," he warned ominously, "We're not going to take pity on you. When we get done, you'll wish you had!"

As they left, Hal knew his face was ashen and his thin lips were trembling. He went into the grocery store mechanically, his mind awhirl. After he had finished his shopping and was walking home Jim Morgan came by.

"Hi, Hal. How're things going? I see you've been shopping."

The new Christian did not reply.

Jim studied his face. "What's the trouble, Hal?" he asked. "Something's the matter."

A look of fear flickered in Hal's eyes, and when he spoke his voice was a tense whisper. "I'm in a tough situation." There was an urgency in Hal's manner.

They walked on in the cold, wintry air. The wind was whipping in from the west, a handful of fine, powdery snow in its teeth. The temperature was so cold the car tires crunched noisily over the packed snow.

Jim turned to his companion now that they were alone. "Now, Hal, what's wrong?"

"I–I haven't said anything about this," Hal began hesitantly, but Pete Nolan and Doug are really pouring it on for me to join their gang."

Jim's eyes widened. "I've been hearing about that gang of theirs. It really sounds rugged. You aren't going to do it, are you?"

Hal shook his head. "I should say not," he said firmly. "Those guys are only headed for trouble. A Christian couldn't get himself involved in the things they're planning to do."

Jim breathed his relief. "I'm sure glad you're not throwing in with them, Hal," he said. "That's the big thing. But if you've already decided against it, that settles it, doesn't it?"

Hal paused momentarily. "They threatened me if I even told anyone about it," he said, "but I didn't make any promises." He took a deep breath. "They told me that if I don't join, they're going to–to beat me up."

The Morgan boy bristled. "If they do, they'll have two of us to handle," Jim retorted loyally. "We'll go everywhere together for a while."

Hal hesitated. "What I really want, Jim, is to have you praying for me."

"Sure thing, Hal. You can count on it. I'll be praying for you every day."

Hal smiled his relief. "That means more to me than anything else."

CHAPTER 4

A VICIOUS ATTACK

When Hal got home from shopping that afternoon, his father was sitting in the living room, a book in his hands. At first Hal's heart quickened at the sight of it. Then he saw that it was not a Bible.

Big Ed looked up. "Kinda late, ain't you?" he demanded, hostility edging his voice.

"I hurried as fast as I could, Dad."

"Didn't I tell you to get home right after goin' to the stores so you could get that work done?" he snorted, "Didn't I?"

Hal nodded wordlessly.

"You act as though you don't think you have to do anything you're told to do around here, young man. I'm going to teach you different if I have to work you over with my belt."

Hal tinged with color. "I–I'm sorry, Dad. I'll get right at it."

Big Ed snorted. "I'm sorry!" he echoed. "That's all I hear out of you these days. I'm sorry! I've just about had my fill of it."

Hal set to work hurriedly. His father watched him for a moment or two and then turned his attention back to the book he was reading. Half an hour or so later when Hal called him to supper, he laid the book – *How to Conquer the Liquor Habit* – on the table beside him.

Big Ed saw his son staring curiously at the title. "The mine superintendent gave this to me yesterday," he explained. His voice grew almost soft. "Quite a book; I think it's going to have a lot of help for me. It's the kind of thing a fella can get his teeth into."

They sat down. As usual Big Ed started to eat immediately, even though Hal bowed his head in silence to ask God's blessing upon the food.

After a time, Hal's dad continued. "The whole thing is will power, Hal," he said. "The writer of this book says that each one of us is the master of his own destiny. All we've got to do is to have will power and we can conquer any habit, regardless of how much hold it has on us."

Hal nodded. "Maybe that's right," he answered, "but Danny says that if a guy has a problem and is a Christian, he can go to God and get help with it. He doesn't have to depend on himself alone. I think that's why guys who can't keep from drinking are able to do so after they've accepted Christ as their Savior."

Big Ed's face grew livid. "Danny says!" he exploded. "That's all you feed me these days. Danny says! Danny says!" He leaned forward. "Well, let me tell you something, Hal Seybold. You'd be a lot better off if you'd never seen that Danny Orlis – and so would I!"

He drew himself up proudly. "I know Orlis is trying to pressure me into fallin' for that Christian business of his. Well, I don't want or need that kind of help! I'm going to get by on my own!" He picked up the book he had been reading and shook it in his son's face. "I'll show you and Orlis and everyone else that I can conquer this little liquor problem I've got. I can do it all by myself. I don't need the help of some weak-kneed religion!"

His lips curled bitterly, and he slumped back into his chair in silence. Hal studied him carefully, the icy lump in his heart growing.

* * *

The forty-eight hours that Pete Nolan and Doug Ellis had given to Hal passed all too quickly. Although they gave no indication that they even knew him when they met him in the halls on Monday, Hal knew they would be waiting for him that evening after school.

When the final bell rang, closing classes for the day, Hal went to his locker and started to get his coat when he saw Doug at the end of the corridor, eyeing him closely. As he saw Jim Morgan approaching, he turned away.

'What's the matter, Hal?" Jim asked.

"O, nothing. I–I think I'll go up to the library for a while," he said uneasily.

"I've got to be getting home right after school tonight. I promised Kay I'd scoop the walks again if it kept snowing."

Hal forced a tired grin. "I'll see you tomorrow." An hour passed while he lingered over the reference books. It was cold outside. There was a chance – just a chance that Doug and Pete would leave. Still, he could hear the ominous threat in their voices.

One by one the other students put away the books and began to leave. Soon the teacher came over to Hal. "I'm sorry, Hal," she said, "but we're going to have to lock up for the night."

Disappointment reflected in his eyes.

"Would you care to check out the book?"

His cheeks paled. "No–no, thank you." He turned wearily and made his way down to the locker. It was already dark outside. In spite of himself the dread within continued to grow.

Suddenly, the color leaped to Hal's cheeks. Perspiration pearled his forehead and his hands and shoulders began to quiver. He took half a step backwards, involuntarily.

Pete Nolan and Doug Ellis advanced upon him, violence in every move. The Nolan boy's big hand lashed out, grasped Hal by the coat collar, and hauled him close. "Well, what's your answer, Seybold?" he demanded angrily. "Are you joining up with us, or aren't you?"

The muscles in Hal's throat tightened in a quick spasm. He shifted his books from one arm to the other and tried, unsuccessfully, to force himself to look directly into their eyes. He was quavering inside uncontrollably, and for an instant he felt that he could not remain standing there but had to turn and flee.

Doug pushed close to him, thrusting out his jaw and jostling Hal defiantly. "We've fooled around all we're goin' to," Doug put in. "You heard Pete. How about it? Are you joining up with us, or aren't you?"

Hal prayed for courage. When he spoke, his voice was calm and firm. "I've already told you that I can't join your gang. There's just no use in talking about it anymore."

Pete Nolan's face went livid with rage. "We gave you this last chance, Seybold. You'd better change your mind right now if you know what's good for you! That's all I can say!"

Hal shook his head. "The answer's still the same. I can't join your gang. I–"

He didn't get to finish what he was saying. Pete struck him savagely across the mouth with the back of his hand. "This'll teach you!"

The force of the blow sent him staggering. While he was still off balance, Doug hit him in the chest. That sent him sprawling into the snow.

"We'll teach you not to turn us down!" Doug's young voice snarled with hatred.

Both boys jumped on top of Hal before he could scramble to his feet and began to pummel him with their fists. Pete grabbed up a handful of snow and rubbed it angrily in Hal's face, saying, "Maybe this'll teach you not to stay out of our gang when we invite you in! Nobody's going to be able to shove us around and get away with it."

Hal tried to guard Iris face as best he could, twisting and kicking in an effort to free himself. But he was no match for them. Their fists drove rhythmically into his face, bruising his cheeks and cutting his lips. There was the taste of blood in his mouth. At last, the heavy beating stopped and they scrambled to their feet. For one long, tormenting minute Hal lay there, staring up at them from between puffed eyelids, while Pete kicked him in the side. "This is just a sample of what we can give you," he grated. "Remember that. And you'll be gettin' it if you tell anyone about this. Do you understand?"

Hal got slowly to his feet as Pete and Doug went swaggering off into the growing darkness. He dusted the snow from his coat and rubbed his hand, uncertainly, over his bruised and bleeding face.

When he reached home his dad was waiting for him angrily. "I thought I told you to come right home after school! What sort of an excuse have you got this time?"

The boy started for the bedroom without speaking.

Big Ed stared at his cut and bruised face. For a moment, the flames of temper in his eyes flickered, then went out. He jumped up and went over to Hal. "Are you hurt bad, boy?" he asked.

Hal rubbed his cheek tenderly. "I–I don't think so.

"Let me look." Big Ed took him over in the light where he examined him carefully. "Who did this to you, Hal?" His voice was laced with anger. "Who was it?"

"I–I'd rather not tell."

His father stared down at him for the space of a minute. "I don't suppose you even fought back!

I suppose you just stood there and took it!" There was disappointment and frustration in his voice.

"But Dad, there were two of them," he protested. "They knocked me down and jumped on me.

Big Ed swore. "You could've fought back!" He expelled his breath slowly. "You could've showed 'em you were a Seybold instead of a–a weakling."

Hal read the look in his father's eyes. Concern had given way to bitter disappointment. That realization was an icy sword that plunged to the hilt into his aching heart. "I–I'm sorry, Dad!"

Big Ed snorted. "I never thought I'd raise a coward for a son. Is this some of that religion business that Danny Orlis has been feedin' you?"

Hal did not reply and Big Ed stormed into the kitchen, "Get yourself cleaned up and get in here and get to work. I ain't doin' all the housework myself."

Hal did as he was told. His dad said nothing more to him all through the meal. And as soon as they had finished eating, Big Ed got to his feet. The Seybold boy questioned, "Where are you going, Dad?"

The older man scowled at him. "None of your business."

Hal saw the bottle in his dad's coat pocket as he went out the door. The ache inside began to grow. It was worse than the cuts and bruises of the beating he had received.

Hal had not intended to go over to Danny's and Kay's that night. He wanted only to go to bed so no one could see what had happened to him. But as soon as he finished the dishes, he got into his jacket and made his way across town to the little house where Danny and Kay lived.

Kay opened the door in response to his knock. "Why, Hal!" she exclaimed, "What has happened to you?" He went inside and took off his coat. "I–I had a little trouble."

Danny eyed him intently. "Did your dad do this?"

The boy shook his head. "Dad wouldn't give me a beating like this," he said. "He–he boxes me around once in a while, but he never really hurts me.

"Who gave you a beating like this?"

The Seybold lad swallowed hard.

"Don't you know, Hal?"

"I–I know, all right." His voice trailed away. "But–"

For the first time Hal saw real anger in Danny's eyes. "I suppose they made you promise not to tell anyone who did it. Is that it?"

Hal shook his head. "T–they threatened me if I did tell on them, but that–that's not why I've decided not to tell. I just don't want to squeal on anyone."

They went over and sat down. "I know how you feel.

But, Hal, you owe it to the other kids who might get the same sort of a beating if you don't tell who did this."

Hal breathed deeply. "I'd never thought of that."

"And you've got to think about the guys who beat you. If they get away with this, they're going to be that much bolder. They might keep on until they get into serious trouble. You have a responsibility to help them see that they can't live reckless, lawless lives without being punished."

Hal rubbed his throat with trembling fingers. "When you put it that way it does seem different."

"It is different."

He took a deep breath. "You don't think I'd be squealing on them?"

"It would be for their own good."

Hal sat up straight and the fright began to leave his eyes.

"But what are you going to do?" Kay Orlis asked.

"I think you should go to the school authorities, Hal," he said, and at least talk it over with them. However, I rather imagine they'll want to call in the police."

For a long while Danny and Kay talked with Hal. At last, he got to his feet and started for the door.

Danny put his arm about his shoulder. "You've made the right decision. It takes a lot more courage to do what you're going to do than it does to remain silent."

Hal Seybold left the Orlis home. His pulse quickened as he left the house and he looked about uncertainly, as though half expecting to see Pete and Doug. But there was no one in sight.

At the end of the block, suddenly the two boys stepped out of the shadows, one on either side of him, and grabbed him by the arm.

"I thought I told you not to go blabbing to anyone! Now we're gonna fix you. But good!"

CHAPTER 5

TO THE RESCUE

As soon as Hal Seybold had left, Kay turned to Danny. Concern drove away her smile. "Danny, do you think you should have let Hal go home alone?"

"I don't know why not."

"What if Pete and Doug followed him out here and waited until he left? There's no telling what they might do to him if they thought he had told us what they had done to him."

The young pilot opened the closet door and got his coat. "Perhaps I had better tag along and see that Hal gets home safely, although I'm sure there's no danger."

He slipped into his heavy jacket and stepped outside, closing the door. The cold winter wind was whistling around the house and lifting the snow to drive it in little clouds across the street. Danny pulled his coat collar more tightly about his throat and hurried along the sidewalk.

It was dark that night – so dark he did not see the boys until he was some fifteen or twenty yards from them. Then he could only make out their shadowy figures. He never could have seen who they were at that distance, but he recognized their voices instantly, and he became very alert at once.

Doug Ellis' shrill, angered tones drifted to him above the whine of the wind. So, you didn't take our warning about keeping your big mouth shut after all!" Doug blustered. "You had to go over and squeal to Danny Orlis like a baby. We'll give you twice what you got the first time."

Danny, now realizing the dangerous plot the boys had planned, stopped for an instant, screened from view by the tall hedge along the walk.

One of the guys grabbed the boy in the middle and jerked him to one side.

"Doug! Let go of me! "Hal cried, "I haven't done anything to you!"

"Lay off, Ellis!" Pete ordered bossily. "I got first crack at him! No one squeals on Pete Nolan and gets away with it!"

Then Danny saw another figure smaller than the others step out of the shadows. He realized instinctively it was Vic Nolan. "Give it to him, Pete!" he said excitedly. "Give it to him! Show him he can't snitch on us!"

The thin voice seemed to trigger Pete. He struck out savagely with his fist, striking Hal full in the mouth. Hal cried out in pain as he went sprawling in the snow. Pete stood over him. "There now!" he grated defiantly. "That'll teach you!"

"And don't you get funny with us again," Vic shrilled, "or my brother'll really beat you up the next time!"

As Pete struck Hal, Danny ran forward. He clamped his big hand on Pete Nolan's shoulder and spun him around. "That's enough of that, young man!" His voice was taut with anger.

Pete's eyes widened fearfully, and he tried to shrink away, but that was impossible. Danny's fingers only clamped the harder. He could not move.

Vic slipped behind Danny and sped along the sidewalk as fast as he could run. Doug slunk a step or two in that direction, as though to break and run the way Vic had, but Danny Orlis stopped him.

"Stay where you are, Doug Ellis!" he ordered, "I want to talk to you."

Doug was trembling. "I–I can go if I want to," he stammered in fright. "I haven't done anything."

"You'll stay right here until I tell you that you can go."

Pete winced. "Let go of me, you big bully. That hurts!"

Danny Orlis was breathing heavily, and for a brief span of time, he did not speak.

"W-w-what are you trying to do?" Pete said, "Y-you're hurting me, I tell you!"

Danny's grip did not relax. "I suppose you think it didn't hurt Hal for you to beat up on him the way you did."

Doug Ellis' voice raised in a shrill tone. "I–I didn't beat up on him, Danny. It wasn't me. I didn't even touch him!"

Pete Nolan joined in. "We didn't beat up on Hal tonight, Mr. Orlis. What Doug's telling you is the truth. Why, we'd never hurt him. He's our friend."

"You guys seem to forget I was back there a minute ago," Danny informed them coldly, "when you threatened him and told him you were going to give him more than you'd given him the first time. I saw you hit him and knock him down. What about that?"

Doug was on the verge of tears. "I–I just thought we were going to have a little fun with Hal, that's all. I–I didn't know Pete was going to hit him just now."

Pete bristled. 'Who was going to hit him? Who was it who kept begging me to give him the first chance at Hal?"

"It isn't going to do either of you any good to try and lie your way out of it. I know what you were doing." Danny relaxed his grip on Pete's shoulder and the boy moved back a step or two, rubbing his shoulder with his other hand. Danny turned to Hal.

"Are you all right, Hal?"

The Seybold boy rubbed his mouth gingerly and glanced over at his two young assailants. "I–I guess so. But I–I'm sure glad you came along when you did, Danny. They were really going to give me a working over."

The young man stared at Doug and Pete. His voice

was still under control, but there was no mistaking his temper. "You guys were so anxious for a fight a couple of minutes ago when you had three against one. What's the trouble now? If you want to fight so bad, why don't you pick on me?"

They cringed but said nothing.

"You're cowards, that's why." He paused momentarily, staring at first one and then the other. "You were really a couple of big shots when the two of you and Vic were talking to Hal. You were tough! As tough as anybody in the province! Now that there's somebody your size or bigger facing up to you, you're as peaceful as a couple of newborn kittens."

Pete retreated half a step.

"That's it, Pete," Danny continued, "That's just about your stripe, turn tail and run!"

Danny took a step or two in his direction and Pete backed off warily. "N-now, Mr. Orlis, you don't dare lay a hand on me. I–I'm not twenty-one yet. I'm a minor. You can be thrown in jail if you hit me."

Danny laughed. "Do you hear how brave they are, Hal? They talk big but they're cowards. There isn't a real backbone in a whole carload of guys like that."

He faced Doug and Pete once more. "You can quit crawling now, guys. I'm not going to touch either one of you."

* * *

When Hal got home that night, his father was sitting in the living room staring sadly at the floor. Big Ed looked up as he entered. "Where've you been?" he wanted to know.

Hal swallowed and rubbed his swollen lip. "O-over to see Danny and Kay."

His father saw his cut lip and got to his feet. "What happened to you?" Hal's lips twitched. "Those guys caught me again."

Big Ed stepped close to him. "What guys?"

Hal looked away. "Just a couple of guys, Dad. They jumped me after I left Danny's."

Big Ed took hold of Hal's shoulder and turned him to the light. "They knocked out a tooth, that's what they did!" Big Ed exclaimed. His face darkened. "Who were they?"

Hal looked up at him in desperation. "I don't want to be a squealer!" Big Ed's voice rose. "Who were they? Answer me!"

Hal felt the color flee from his cheeks. "Pete Nolan and Doug Ellis."

"Are they the only ones?"

"Vic Nolan was along, but he–he didn't do much."

For a minute or two Big Ed stood there breathing heavily. Then he went for his coat.

"What are you going to do, Dad?"

Big Ed did not answer him. Instead, he stormed out and slammed the door.

Hal stayed up until his Father came home. Big

Ed was still mad. It was easy to see by the way he came striding up on the porch and stomped inside. He glared at Hal. "Why aren't you in bed where you belong?" he demanded.

The boy eyed him uncertainly. "I–I wouldn't have been able to sleep anyway, Dad. I had to stay up and see where you went, and–and what you did."

Big Ed's lips curled bitterly. "It's none of your business what I did!" he snarled. "I don't have to answer to you for what I do and what I don't do."

"You were so mad when you left here, Dad–" His voice trailed away.

"And I'm still mad!" He strode over to a chair and dropped into it! "I fixed things! But good!" he exclaimed. "If those kids think they can knock a Seybold around and bust a tooth for him, they've got another guess comin'!"

Concern leaped to Hal's eyes. "What did you do, Dad?"

"What any dad would do." He strutted around the room. "I went down to the cops and filed charges against 'em! We'll show 'em!"

"You didn't!"

"That's exactly what I did! Do you know what it'll cost to get that tooth of yours fixed? Fifty bucks! What do you think – that I'm made of money?"

"But, Dad," Hal protested, "the guys'll blame me for it! They'll all be down on me when they find out that you turned them in."

Big Ed jerked himself upright. "Listen, you! Shut your mouth and get to bed, or I'll knock another tooth out for you!"

Hal retreated to his bedroom silently.

The next morning when he got to school, Doug Ellis and the Nolan brothers were standing on the steps of the school waiting for him. Vic sneered at him. "Look who's coming!" he jeered. "The little tattletale! The baby who has to run for help just because he gets shoved around a little."

Pete turned to Doug. "Am I ever glad we found out what a coward Hal is before we considered him in our plans."

"That's for sure," Doug continued. "We wouldn't take him in now if he got down on his knees and begged us."

Hal moved as though to go past. Pete glanced up and down the playground to be sure no one was watching and stepped in front of him, shoving him hard with his open hand. "Not so fast, Seybold. Not so fast. We're not through talking to you yet."

Vic stepped closer, eagerly. "Hit him, Pete! Hit him again! Show him what he gets when he tattles on us! Show him he can't get away with it!"

"That's just what I've got a notion to do."

The muscles in Hal's throat tightened and perspiration pearled his forehead. His lips parted, but before he could speak the city police car drove up in front of the school and a tall, uniformed officer got out.

Doug Ellis' eyes widened and he turned to his companions. "There's a cop, Pete! What do you suppose he wants?"

Neither Nolan boy answered. Motionless, they stared at the officer, until he approached them.

"You're Douglas Ellis and the Nolan brothers, aren't you?"

They nodded wordlessly, their voices choking in their throats.

"We'd like to have a little talk with you down at the station. I think you'd better come with me."

Pete shook his head and took half a step backward. Vic started to cry.

"B-b-but we've got to go to school," Pete protested.

"Mr. Garber already knows about this. We called him from headquarters before we left."

Fear stood full in Doug's eyes. "But we haven't done anything. There must be some mistake. We haven't done anything."

Nevertheless, the officer escorted them to the police car and drove off toward the station with them. Hal stared after them in anguish.

CHAPTER 6

DAD'S ADVICE

Hal suffered through the next two days at school. Neither Doug Ellis nor the Nolan brothers came back to school, but the Seybold boy was miserable. The story of how they had beaten Hal and the fact that his dad had filed charges against them spread rapidly throughout the school. Several guys stopped him in the corridor and talked with him about it. "Your face is sure a mess. Did they knock that tooth out?" His mouth tightened. "I'd just as soon not talk about it." He walked away, leaving them standing there.

That evening Jim Morgan met him in the hall after school and they went home together. "I hear that your dad filed charges against the Nolans and Doug," Jim said. "Is that right?"

Hal nodded. "I tried to talk him out of it, but it didn't do any good. Now everybody in school thinks I'm a squealer and a baby." There was a short silence.

"You won't have to worry about what Pete and Doug might do to you, Hal," Jim said, "I'll walk home with you for a couple of weeks. Danny says they're cowards. They'll never tackle two of us together."

He rubbed his swollen mouth tenderly. "I don't know why I'm the one who always gets in such messes," he said. "But I can tell you one thing – if it hadn't been for those times of Bible reading and prayer I've had with you, I don't know how I'd take all this. I'd probably have lost my temper over it like I did before."

Jim smiled his approval.

When Hal got home that evening, his dad was already there, sprawled in a chair. Big Ed glanced up as his son entered. His face was flushed, and his eyes were bloodshot. "Now, where've you been?" he demanded. His words slurred.

Hal bit his lower lip and strove to keep his voice from trembling. "Dad, you promised me that you wouldn't drink anymore."

Big Ed Seybold struggled to an upright position and leered at him. "Who're you to tell me what I can do and what I can't do? Since when do I have to come and ask you if I decided that I want a little drink? I'm your dad, remember?"

Concern tightened Hal's throat and flickered in his eyes. "But, Dad," he exclaimed, "you know what they told you at the mine about drinking. You'll get fired if they find out that you've started to drink again. And this time you won't get back. The super-intendent said it would be for good."

Big Ed breathed heavily, and his lips curled. "Now, why don't you run down to the mine office and tattle on me, Hal, the way you went trotting over to Danny Orlis the other night?"

Hal's lips trembled. For an instant, his temper flared, but he said nothing. Big Ed, however, was not ready to stop.

"This whole mess is Danny Orlis' fault, the way I figure."

"But, Dad," Hal said, "all Danny did was come out and stop them from beating me up."

His dad eyed him darkly. "Sure, that's what you say. But why were you out that night in the first place? You'd gone over to see Danny Orlis and tell him all about it." Anger whitened Big Ed's face. "I was home," he continued. "You could've talked to me about it. But no! You had to go over and see Orlis! You had to cry on his shoulder! I don't know as I blame Doug and the Nolans for gettin' teed off at you. I'd have done the same thing myself."

Hal searched for words to explain, but they would not come out.

"You should've stood up and taken your beatin' like a man!"

Choking back the tears, Hal took off his coat and cap and hung them in the closet. That accomplished, he pivoted to face his dad cautiously because he knew how quickly his dad's temper would explode when he had been drinking.

Big Ed's voice rose triumphantly. "I've been doin' a lot of thinkin', Hal! I made a mistake filin' charges against them kids! I decided I should've let you solve your own problems!"

Hal stared at him incredulously. "You–you mean you're not going to press charges against them?" he echoed.

"I called up the police tonight and told them I wanted to get that paper I'd signed – that I wasn't going to have anything to do with that mess!"

"You mean they–they won't be taken to court and tried?"

Big Ed's face burst into a grin. "Now, don't that make you feel bad?"

"Make me feel bad? No! I think it's great!"

Big Ed stared at him. "Well! Maybe there's some hope for you, yet!"

Hal got ready for school half an hour earlier than usual the next morning. His dad, fighting a terrific headache, was short-tempered and in a sour mood.

"Now, if those guys give you a bad time on the way to school this morning, show them what you're made of," he ordered. "Be tough! Whale right in and let them know that you're Big Ed Seybold's kid and you ain't takin' anything off nobody."

Hal got into his coat.

"Did-ja hear me?"

His son nodded. "They're not going to give me any more trouble," Hal said. "You don't have to worry about that."

"I ain't worryin' about it. I'm just tellin' you what to do if it happens. When I was a kid your age, they all walked a block out of the way to keep from crossin' me! I wasn't scared of none of 'em. I didn't care how big they was."

Hal picked up his books and started for the door, but his father stopped him. "The only way to get along in this world is to be tough. Be tougher than the guy who wants to step on your toes. That's the way I do." He came over to where Hal was standing. "I'll tell you what you do," he went on. "Come home tonight and I'll give you a couple of lessons! I'll show you how to take care of yourself when guys bigger than you try to walk on you!" He grinned darkly. "I've got some tricks of using your knees and elbows and even your teeth that they never thought of." His face grew angry at the thought of what had happened to Hal. "I'm not goin' to have a kid of mine licked by anybody. I don't care if there was two of 'em and they're both bigger'n you."

He nodded vigorously. "I know a few tricks that'll even up the odds! How about it, Hal? Are you game?"

The boy lifted his gaze to meet his father's. "But, Dad," he protested, "I don't want to fight Pete and Doug. I don't want to fight anybody."

Big Ed brushed aside his objection. "That's just because you're scared. When I get done teachin' you,

Hal, there won't be a kid in the whole town who'll dare to mix it up with you." He took a deep breath. "Now, mind what I told you!" Big Ed ordered. "You get yourself home right after school! We've got some work to do. I'll help you with the dishes and the housework, and then we'll get busy."

Hal left the house and went out to the sidewalk and headed for the school. He was half a block away when his dad called to him. "Hal, don't say anything to anyone about that deal of ours. That's our little secret!"

The Seybold boy did not have long to think about his father and what would happen at home that night. On the steps of the school Pete Nolan and Doug Ellis stopped him. Pete surveyed him critically, a sneer on his young face. "I knew you were just a big bluff, Seybold," he snarled.

Doug laughed cockily. "Thought you had us scared, didn't you? I guess we showed you!"

Pete shook him strongly. "If we wanted to, we could give you a good working over right here in broad daylight! That's what you deserve, tryin' to get us in trouble the way you did. We should give you a good beating right here in front of everybody and show the rest of these pansies they'd better not cause any trouble for us."

Hal raised his eyes to stare at them evenly. "I'm not afraid of you." His voice was firm.

Jim came up just then, his fists knotted. "Hal, need any help?"

The Seybold boy laughed. 'With these guys? They run in packs! They're afraid of a fair fight."

His eyes darkened. "Now get out of my way!" He stepped forward slowly, but without hesitation.

Pete and Doug fell back, while Hal and Jim went past them and on up the school steps.

When they were in the school building Jim turned, admiring his companion. "What happened to you?" he exclaimed.

"I just got tired of taking that stuff. That's all! I'm not going to take it anymore!"

CHAPTER 7

A TERRIBLE DISAPPOINTMENT

The young people's society at church had a calendar of activities, and the one that attracted the most interest was the scavenger hunt. Ever since it was announced, everyone began to look forward to it eagerly.

Two or three weeks before the big event, a publicity committee was appointed, and plans for the scavenger hunt continued rapidly. It was all very secret with Danny and Kay and the minister's wife working out the lists and planning the lunch. With all the secrecy, the excitement built.

Hal had been thinking so much about the coming young people's party that he had almost forgotten about Pete and Doug until they stopped bum in the corridor after school.

His eyes narrowed. "Get out of my way!" He spoke softly, but with unmistakable firmness.

Pete laughed uneasily. "Don't get so huffy," he said. "I don't know what's got into you lately. We're your friends, remember? You don't need to act as though you want a fight."

"I don't want a fight," the Seybold boy continued. "I just don't plan on being shoved around anymore."

Doug put his hands in his pocket and slouched against the locker. "We just want to talk to you, Hal," he said.

Hal relaxed a little. "What do you want to talk with me about?"

Doug and Pete glanced at one another. "I don't know whether we should tell him or not, do you, Doug?" Pete asked.

"Not the way he's acting."

"I don't know that I'd be interested in hearing anything you've got to say." He shifted his books from one arm to the other. "I've got to hurry. I've got things to do."

Neither of them made a move to stop him. He walked past them and went striding down the steps and out into the cold winter air.

That night when he got home, he tried to talk to his father about them and what they had said, but Big Ed refused to listen.

"It ain't talk that'll make guys like that respect you. It's what you can do with your fists. Beat 'em up a couple of times and they'll be plenty glad to leave you alone. And respect you, too."

He started to unbutton his shirt. "Get your shirt off, Hal. I want to give you another lesson. Somethin' tells me it ain't goin' to be long until you'll need everything I been teachin' you."

"But, Dad, I am worried," he said. "I don't know what Pete and Doug are going to do, but it's not going to be with their fists. They even told me that." He breathed deeply. "They said I'd know it was them, but I wouldn't be able to do anything about it."

"All you've got to do is follow the directions I been givin' you, and you'll be able to do plenty about it! Come on, Hal! Show a little life. Remember that you're Big Ed Seybold's son, and you're as tough as anyone in town!"

* * *

Ordinarily the young people's parties came and went without creating any special interest at school. But the scavenger hunt was different. As soon as word of it got around, the students began to ask about receiving invitations. Notices were put up on the bulletin board that everyone was invited.

Jim Morgan was pleased by the interest, but he couldn't understand it. "Other places I've been, we've had scavenger hunts," he said, "I always enjoyed them, but I didn't think they were as much fun as everyone lets on."

Hal shook his head. "I don't know how the talk

got started that it was really going to be something special, Jim. But I think word of the kind of parties Danny and Kay have helped us put on has been getting around. Not many of the kids have been on a scavenger hunt and it sounds exciting."

"It will be exciting, too. I can tell you that much."

Hal didn't even know that Doug and Pete were waiting around to talk to him until Jim went on. When the Morgan boy was out of sight, they came out from behind a tall hedge and caught up with him.

"Just a minute, Seybold," Pete said, "We want to talk to you. Doug tells me you're having a big party over at the church you go to."

Hal's eyes brightened. "It is going to be a big party. Just about the biggest we've ever had. And it sounds like it's going to be a lot of fun, too. Are you guys coming?"

Doug laughed shortly. "We haven't decided yet.

"This scavenger hunt is going to be a great time," Hal continued. "I can tell you that much right now. I've never been to one, but I know it's going to be great."

Pete chuckled. "Believe it or not," he said, "but I've never been to a church party. Now, what do you think of that?"

"I think you should come. I think you both should. You'd find out how much fun we have at young people's."

When Hal got home from school that night, his father was sitting at the dining room table reading the book his superintendent had given him. Hal saw the tension in his face. "Why don't you go over and talk to Danny, Dad?" he suggested. "He can help you. I know he can!"

Big Ed snorted. "What's the use of me going over and talking to him? If I need help, I'll get it from a real man."

Hal felt his throat tighten. The color fled from his cheeks. "But, Dad, he can help you. Lots of guys have gone to Danny for help with their problems. He'd understand."

His father got to his feet and closed the book noisily. "How many times do I have to tell you that I don't need no help? I can take care of myself. I can whip a little thing like a bottle if I want to."

Even as he spoke, Hal noticed that his dad's tongue was thick and his words slurred. He had been drinking again.

"Come on, now!" Big Ed ordered. "You and I have got some things to do. I want to give you another lesson. You've got to show those kids just how tough a Seybold is!"

The boy's eyes filled with scalding tears. They surged up under his eyelids and quivered there.

Big Ed saw them. "What's the blubberin' about?"

Hal stared at him miserably, then turned and fled to his bedroom and shut the door. For an instant he stood there, hand on the knob, his body resting against the door.

His dad stormed into the kitchen and sat down.

Hal sank to his knees in prayer – a prayer that was more than words. It was the cry of an anguished heart.

Although he tried to pretend that it wasn't true, he realized that his dad was drinking more than he had for many weeks. Big Ed was sullen and morose. When his father entered the house, he looked around critically, hunting for something that was wrong.

"Don't you ever pay any attention to me, Hal?" he demanded. "I told you to do them dishes first! What's the matter with you? Can't you understand plain English?"

"But, Dad–"

Big Ed's face grew livid. "That's right! Sass me! It doesn't make any difference what I say. I'm just your father. Go right ahead and do as you please!"

Hal stared at him helplessly. "I want to do things the way you want me to. Dad," he said. "I was just going to tell you that I understood you to say you wanted me to scrub the kitchen floor just as soon as I got home from school. So that's what I did. I've got water heating for the dishes."

Big Ed's lips curled. "I told you to scrub, all right. But whoever heard of scrubbin' first? You were supposed to scrub after you got the dishes done!" His voice rose. "I don't know why I even bother tellin' you what I want done. You do just as you please anyway! If that's what bein' a Christian is, I sure don't want any part of it!"

Hal choked back his temper and, praying for

control, he went to the sink. He wanted to tell his dad about the scavenger hunt and to ask him if it was all right if he planned on going. But every time he thought of it, Big Ed was in a foul temper.

He talked with Jim about it on the way to school the morning of the party. "I sure want to go if I can," he said, "but I don't know whether I'll be able to go or not. Dad has been rough to get along with lately." He paused and breathed deeply. "Don't say anything to anyone about it, but Dad has been drinking again."

The Morgan boy nodded understandingly. "I know what that's like," he said. "I used to have it around home a lot before I came to live with the Orlises." Then he smiled. "Of course, my dad's a Christian now."

"I wonder if that will ever happen at our house?"

They crossed the street in silence. "That's tough about the scavenger hunt. Do you think it would make any difference if I went and asked your dad for you?"

Hal shook his head. "That would only make things worse. I'll have to do the talking to him, but I almost know what he'll say before I ask him."

He could scarcely wait for school to get out that night. He dashed home and flew into the work faster than he had ever done before. When his father came home, he had cleaned the house, made the beds and was just finishing the dishes.

Big Ed forgot his question and dropped heavily. Hal greeted him with a smile. "Hi, Dad," he sang out, "how did it go today?"

His dad frowned. "That was a stupid question. It was hard, dirty work and I'm tired. Does that answer your question?"

He ripped off his coat and flung it carelessly over a chair.

"I've got supper almost ready, Dad," he said. "I put it on the stove while I was doing the dishes. We can eat by the time you get washed up."

Big Ed eyed him suspiciously. "Now what are you up to?" he asked. What have you done this time?" His mouth tightened. "Or is it somethin' you want to do?"

Hal hesitated. All he would have to do would be to get his coat and cap after dinner and go out as if he were going to the library or over to see one of the guys to study, and his father wouldn't say a thing. The chances were he wouldn't even ask where he was going.

But Hal couldn't do that now. Even if he didn't actually tell a lie, it would be deceiving his dad, and that would be just as bad.

Big Ed forgot his question and dropped heavily to a kitchen chair, railing against the superintendent out at the mine. "The next time that super pops off at me, I'm going to let him have it!"

Hal was scarcely listening. He felt the muscles in his throat tighten and perspiration beaded his forehead. He tried several times to talk to his dad, but it was not until they were seated at the table that he dared.

"Dad, I'd like to ask you something," he began.

"I might have known it! You never do anything the way you're supposed to unless you want something!"

"I was just wondering if – I could go on the scavenger hunt tonight."

Big Ed's forehead wrinkled. "Scavenger hunt?" he demanded. "Who's putting that on?" His scowl deepened. "I'll bet Orlis has something to do with it."

"Danny and Kay are sponsoring the young people's society, but the party isn't at their place. We'll start at the church and go all over town collecting things. It'll be a lot of fun!"

His father snorted. "I can guess how much fun it'll be!" He took a deep breath. "If Orlis has anything to do with it, you're not going. Do you hear me?"

Hal's heart sank. "But Dad, all the kids in town are going."

"All of them except one!" He leaned back in his chair.

Hal sighed wearily. Suddenly he didn't even feel like eating. Doug and Pete were going to be at the scavenger hunt! He might have a chance to talk to them about the Lord. If he was there, he might be able to talk them into coming to the meetings all the time. His heart ached. After a moment or two he pushed away from the table and went to the phone. His father saw him.

"Now just what do you think you're a-goin' to do, young man?"

"Jim and I were going to the scavenger hunt together," he said. "I was just going to tell him that I can't be there tonight."

Big Ed laughed mirthlessly. "Get away from that phone! He'll find out you ain't a-goin' when you don't show up. You don't need to call him." Hal glanced up at the clock. It was almost time for the scavenger hunt to start. The kids would be gathering in the basement of the church and Danny and Kay would be organizing them into teams. Everybody would be there. Everybody, that is, except him. His lower lip trembled with self-pity.

At that moment there was a knock at the door, and Big Ed stumbled to his feet. "I'll answer the door! You get into that bedroom and get to studyin' before I lose my temper!"

Jim was at the door. Glaring at him, Big Ed stepped outside. "What do you want?"

"Hal was going to meet me at the corner. He didn't show up, so I came over to get him."

"Hal's not here!"

Jim's eyes reflected his astonishment. "Not here? Did he go to the scavenger hunt?"

Big Ed swore. "How would I know? He lies to me all the time."

Jim took a deep breath. "But he said that he'd go with me tonight. I wonder what happened?"

Mr. Seybold snorted indignantly. "Don't ask me about that boy! I'm about to give up on him! Now get out of here and leave me alone!"

CHAPTER 8

BIG EXCITEMENT

Hal went to bed shortly after his father left the house, but he lay for a long while thinking about the scavenger hunt. After a while he dropped off to sleep, restlessly.

The next morning when he got up his father was grumping around the kitchen trying to fix breakfast. "Now see that you stay away from that Orlis guy, Hal," Big Ed ordered.

When Hal got to school a few minutes before the bell, the kids were standing around in excited little knots, talking softly. He looked at them and the ache within him grew. They were talking about the scavenger hunt and how much fun they had. That was sure.

He started past them, but someone called out to him. "Hal, did you hear the news?"

The excitement in his voice kindled an excitement in the Seybold boy. "Mason's drugstore was robbed last night!"

"That's right! And whoever did it got over a hundred dollars!"

He stared at his companions as though he could not believe what they were saying. His eyes widened. "You're kidding!"

Someone else, who heard the guys talking as he was passing by, stopped and turned back momentarily. "No, Hal, they're not kidding. Someone did break into the drugstore last night."

Hal shook his head in disbelief. "They used a crowbar, a tire iron, or something sharp on one end to force open one of the back windows."

The night cop found that the store had been robbed when he made his first rounds before midnight, so it was done early," someone else said, "probably while our scavenger hunt was going on."

The students left their lockers and walked slowly down the corridor to their home rooms.

"Mr. Mason said the thieves must have known where the money was hidden because the only things that were pulled out were the aspirins on the third shelf. And that's where the money was."

Hal breathed deeply. "Almost everybody knows where he keeps his money."

His companion nodded. "I hadn't thought of that, but I guess you're right."

The Seybold boy sat down in his seat and started to put his books away. "Wasn't anything else taken?"

"Just the money and two boxes of candy bars. They think the place was robbed by someone here at school."

Hal caught his breath.

"And that's not all. One of the thieves left a very incriminating piece of evidence in the store."

For some reason Hal kept thinking of the robbery at various times throughout the day. It was still foremost in his mind when he came out of the school building that afternoon and found Jim Morgan waiting for him.

"Hi, Hal. We missed you on the scavenger hunt last night."

"I asked Dad, but he wouldn't let me go."

Jim eyed him a little suspiciously. He had been over to the Seybold house for Hal the night before, but Big Ed had said that Hal sneaked out earlier in the evening and he didn't know where he had gone. And that was the night the drugstore had been robbed! A dark, ugly thought slipped into Jim's mind. But no! Hal couldn't have had anything to do with that! He was a Christian now! Everybody knew about his fine testimony, and his determination to live a separated fife. Still Big Ed had been furious when Jim appeared at the house and asked for Hal. What reason would he have to lie about his son being home? Jim felt sick inside.

Hal looked his way curiously. "What's the matter, Jim?" he asked. "Don't you feel good?"

That evening at home Jim brought up the subject to Danny and Kay. They had both heard about it.

"Kay and I were just talking about it when you came in, Danny said. "It was on the radio this morning. Makes a person feel terrible to think something like that would happen here in Gluymon." He took a deep breath. "To be real honest with you, I've been afraid something like this would happen."

Jim studied him intently. "What do you mean?" he asked.

Danny smiled. "I'm not exactly sure."

"Do–do you think Doug and Pete had anything to do with it?"

The young pilot was slow in answering. "I wouldn't want to accuse anyone, Jim."

"I thought of them right away, but they couldn't have had anything to do with it. They were at the scavenger hunt last night."

Danny's forehead crinkled. "That's right, they were. I'd almost forgotten about that." He turned towards Kay. "It's like Kay always says. We shouldn't jump to conclusions about anyone. Something like this happens, and unless we're careful, we try to figure things out. And the chances are we wind up talking about someone when we don't know anything about it."

Jim was silent momentarily. "Just the same, I'm glad Hal isn't in with those guys anymore."

Something about the tone in Jim's voice attracted Kay's attention. "But, Jim, it wouldn't make any difference if Hal were in with Doug and Pete or not as far as Mason's drugstore is concerned. He's consecrated his life to Christ. He wouldn't be involved in any-thing like that."

"No, I guess not," he said, doubt edging his voice.

* * *

At the Seybold house Hal was washing the supper dishes when his father came in. Big Ed muttered an answer to his greeting and dropped heavily into a chair.

"You still foolin' around with them dishes?" he demanded. "I thought I told you to come right home from school and get to work. Don't you pay any 'tention to what I say anymore?"

Hal did not turn around. "I did come right home from school."

His father snorted. "You're lyin' to me again. You probably went sneakin' over to see that blasted Orlis guy! And after I told you not to!" He swore savagely. "Sometime I'm goin' to lose my temper with you and tear you apart!"

Hal flushed hotly but did not reply. It was several minutes before Big Ed spoke again. "Now maybe you'll see that I know what I'm doin' when I won't let you go to nothin' at that church no more."

Hal half turned to face him. "What do you mean, Dad?"

"Take that scavenger hunt, or whatever you call it. It was a mighty good thing for you, I wouldn't let you go out last night."

"Why?"

Big Ed's voice rose. Why? Don't tell me you don't know why – after what happened at Mason's drugstore last night."

"But what would the scavenger hunt have had to do with it?"

Big Ed got up heavily and crossed to another chair on the other side of the room. "All those kids were out roamin' around on the streets last night instead of bein' home where they belonged," he said. "If you'd been with them, the chances are they'd be thinkin' maybe you had something to do with it."

"But Dad, the kids were all together. They couldn't have done anything without the others knowing about it."

Big Ed slouched in the chair and crossed his legs lazily. "That's not the way I got it. The guys in the mine were talkin' about it this mornin'. Those kids were runnin' all over town last night a-pestering' people for stuff like an old shaving mug or a buggy whip. It wouldn't have taken no time at all for a couple of them to have slipped out and broke into that store, figgerin' on a perfect alibi." He expelled his breath slowly. "No, sir," he insisted. "I really done you a favor when I wouldn't let you go out with Orlis last night!"

CHAPTER 9

POLICE QUESTIONINGS

For the next two or three days all that anyone in Gluymon, Ontario, heard was talk of the drugstore robbery. At night when Danny returned from his flying job at the mine, Kay and Jim filled him in on the latest developments.

"They're really going after things, Danny," Jim said. "According to the kids at school they've checked that store from one end to the other, just like the big city detectives do when they want to solve a crime. The police were out to the school again today talking to some of the guys."

Kay took a slice of bread, then passed the plate to Danny. "It makes me a little sick even to think that some young person might have broken into the drugstore."

Danny nodded thoughtfully. "I don't see how money could mean that much to anyone, do you?"

The police had been to the school several times since the robbery, talking with the principal and some of the guys. Hal was surprised one morning when a girl appeared at the door of his home room and said he was wanted in the principal's office.

He hurried down the hall to the little office at the far end of the building.

Mr. Garber was sitting behind his big desk when Hal entered, and the chief of police was in a chair close by.

"Did–did you want to see me, Mr. Garber?" he asked.

The principal nodded coldly. "Chief Clark would like to ask you a few questions."

The boy cleared his throat. "Y-y-yes sir."

There was a momentary silence. "Now, Hal," the chief of police began. "We would like to know where you were, and what you were doing the night Mr. Mason's drugstore was robbed."

Hal tried to look the chief squarely in the eye, but somehow, he could not. And when he spoke his voice was choked and hesitant. "I was home."

"All evening?"

"I wanted to go to the scavenger hunt, but Dad wouldn't let me."

The chief pursed his lips, and taking a pencil from his pocket tapped it absent-mindedly against his finger. "I suppose you can prove that if it becomes necessary?" Chief Clark asked.

Hal caught his breath sharply. The look in the chief s eyes and the tone in his voice was alarming.

"You can ask my dad if you don't believe me," Hal said, "or Jim Morgan. They can tell you."

The chief made a note in his book. "You have been in Mason's drugstore quite a lot, haven't you?"

"Sure I have," Hal said. "Everybody goes to Mason's drugstore."

"Did you know where he keeps the money hidden when he goes home at night?"

Hal swallowed hard. "Everybody knows where Mr. Mason keeps his money."

Mr. Clark's mouth firmed. "I see. Then you were aware of the fact that he left the money in the store overnight?"

Hal ran his fingers through his hair. "Like I said, everybody knew it."

There was a short silence. "What would you say if I told you that we just talked with Jim?" the chief asked. "He said he had stopped over at your place that evening a few minutes before the party. He asked your dad where you were, and he told him that you weren't at home, that he didn't know where you were."

Hal's eyes widened and everything blurred. For an instant he opened his mouth in desperation, but he could not speak. "I was at home all the time, Mr. Clark," he protested. "I didn't go out at all."

Chief Clark straightened. "Are you saying that Jim Morgan lied to us?"

Hal faltered.

"Then you weren't at home that night after all?" The words lashed out, savagely.

Hal stared at the speaker miserably. "Yes, I–I was home. Honest, I was."

"First you tell us that you were home. Then you say Jim didn't lie when he said you weren't at home. How do you explain that?"

Hal shook his head. His mind spun and the words he wanted to come out forcefully and confidently were hesitant instead. "I–I don't know how to explain it. I know Jim Morgan wouldn't lie, but I didn't leave the house at all that night. I swear it!"

The chief of police found his gaze and forced him to look at him. "It would be much easier for you if you would tell us exactly what you did that night, Hal. If you don't, I'm afraid it will go hard with you."

Hal looked over at Mr. Garber, desperately. "What can I do to make Mr. Clark know that I'm telling the truth?"

"If you are telling the truth, Hal," the principal said, "you will be able to find evidence to prove it.

There was a brief silence which seemed like an hour to Hal. Then the chief of police reached into his pocket quite deliberately and extracted a heavy woolen glove. "Have you ever seen this before, Hal?"

Hal moistened his lips. "That glove belongs to me, Mr. Clark," he said lamely. "I've wondered where I lost it."

The silence was electric. "We found this glove in Mason's drugstore the morning after the robbery.

As a matter of fact, we found it just inside the back window where the thieves entered!"

Hal left the principal's office, his mind reeling. His glove had been found at the drugstore! His glove! And now Chief Clark and Mr. Garber were sure that he had been one of the guys who had broken into the drugstore and stolen the money!

A sick, numb feeling swept over him.

Almost without realizing what he was doing during the rest of the day at school, he walked home and went into the house. His father was waiting for him. Big Ed jumped to his feet angrily and jerked his big gold watch from his pocket.

"What's the matter with you?" he demanded. "Don't you know when you're supposed to be home?"

Hal's lower lip quivered and he fought to control it.

Big Ed swore angrily. "Answer me or I'll bash you one!

"I–I'm sorry, Dad. I had to go to the principal's office." The words choked off conclusively. "It took you a long time to think up that excuse."

"I–I'm telling you the truth, Dad."

His dad snorted his decision. "If you're tellin' me the truth, young man, it's the first time you've done it since you started messin' around with that Orlis fella."

Hal choked and hot, scalding tears came to his eyes. He turned quickly away. His dad slumped back into his chair.

"Since you don't know enough to come home from school when you're supposed to, you're not goin' to church for a couple of weeks," Big Ed ordered. "You can do your work on Sunday morning. And I don't want to catch you sneakin' over there, either – understand?"

Hal heard what he was saying, but the words did not register. All he knew was that he was suspected of breaking into Mason's drugstore. He tried to pray but couldn't. He worked around the house mechanically, too stunned even to think. He wanted to talk with his father or Jim about what had happened, and what the chief of police had said to him. But he could not. Somehow, he could not tell anyone.

That night sleep would not come. The chief hadn't arrested him even though he had found his glove in the drugstore, but Hal knew that was coming at any time. Perhaps it would happen the next morning before he finished breakfast, or at night before he could get back to the house from school again.

Hal went to classes as usual the next morning, but his mind was not on his studies. The words swam before his eyes and the harsh, accusing voice of the police chief still rang in his ears. No one said anything to him about having been called into the principal's office for questioning. However, it seemed to Hal that everyone must know about it. He felt that he could see it in their faces.

That morning Mr. Garber sent for Jim Morgan. Again the chief of police was with him.

"I know we talked with you yesterday, James," the chief said, "but there are some more things we would like to check out."

Jim squirmed uncomfortably. "I–I've already told you everything I know about what happened that night."

The chief ignored what he said. "We contacted the authorities in Iron Mountain, Colorado, and in Warroad, Minnesota. We learned you have been in trouble before."

Jim Morgan felt the color drain from his cheeks. "That was before I became a Christian."

The chief pursed his lips. "Frankly, the evidence we have been able to gather points to you and Hal Seybold."

Jim stared at him in disbelief. "But–but we weren't even together that night!" he protested.

The officer chose his words with care. "I know that is what you both say, and I would like to believe you, but we cannot ignore the evidence we've been able to find. You could have slipped away from the scavenger hunt for a few minutes, met Hal Seybold long enough to have broken into the drugstore, taken the money, and gotten back before anyone was suspicious."

Jim's face paled. For an instant he had difficulty in controlling his voice enough to speak. "But I didn't, Mr. Clark. I was on the scavenger hunt all the time, and I didn't even see Hal that night. That's the truth!"

The chief consulted his notes. "After the leader divided the party into groups for the scavenger hunt, you insisted on going after several of the items alone. And the last one took you longer than anyone else. In fact, they had already started to eat lunch when you came back."

The Morgan boy straightened, and his voice raised slightly. "Did you ever try to catch a live sparrow?"

Mr. Clark did not smile. "You could very well have met Hal Seybold somewhere, broken into the drugstore and taken what you wanted, and still returned to the scavenger hunt."

Jim sighed oddly. "I–I've been telling you the truth, Mr. Clark."

The chief of police leaned forward. "Can you prove it?"

The boy hesitated. "I–I don't know."

Mr. Clark continued to question him for half an hour or more, going over the same subjects again and again. But the Morgan boy's story did not change.

At last the chief got to his feet. "Since we haven't finished our investigation yet, James, we aren't in position to make any arrests. For your sake, I sincerely hope that what you are telling me is true."

Jim was trembling violently when he left Mr. Garber's private office.

CHAPTER 10

A HEART SOFTENS

Big Ed Seybold had just pushed himself back from the supper table when there was a brisk knock at the door. He took another slice of bread and buttered it deliberately. The knock came again.

He turned his head. "Hal! Hal!

A moment later the boy came to the bedroom door, his history book in his hand. "Did you want something, Dad?" He tried to mask the concern that troubled every waking moment.

"There's someone at the door! Go and see who it is.

Hal laid aside his book and started for the door.

"But remember, you're not a-goin' over to Orlises or the church either."

When Hal opened the door Chief Clark came in. The boy swallowed hard.

Big Ed squirmed around in his chair. When he

saw who it was, he angrily got to his feet. "What're you doin' here?" he demanded.

The chief closed the door behind him. "There are times, Ed, when I have to do things that I don't particularly like to do."

"Like what?"

"I've got to talk to you about Hal."

Big Ed bristled.

Briefly the chief told him what had taken place. When he finished the big man snorted at the charge. "Hal didn't do it."

"I wish I could be as sure of that as you are, Ed."

"I don't care what evidence you've got!" His temper began to build. "I know my boy. I know he didn't break into no drugstore!"

Chief Clark straightened slowly. "Now, Ed, I didn't come over here to argue with you. We have the evidence. We can prove what Hal and his pal have done."

Big Ed Seybold shook his head defiantly. "You don't have no evidence to prove that Hal broke into that drugstore," he retorted.

The chief continued, his voice calm. "We have more evidence than you think. We know, for instance, that he told us he was at home that night. And we know that you told Jim Morgan he wasn't home and you didn't have any idea where he was or when he would be home."

Big Ed Seybold hunched forward, his eyes peering intently into the eyes of the officer.

"I'm goin' to tell you somethin' and it's the plain truth, Clark. Hal didn't lie about bein' out of the house that night. I was the one who lied to Jim Morgan."

Unbelief gleamed in the chief's eyes.

"I know you think I'm covering up for Hal, but I'm not. The truth is Hal was here all night."

"Now, Ed, do you honestly expect me to believe that?"

The big miner's mouth tightened, and his fists clenched until the cords stood out on the backs of his hands. "Hal ain't like me, and he ain't like his mother was. He ain't even like he used to be a few months ago."

"Now, what do you mean by that?"

"He's a Christian now, and there's been a big change in the way he studies and works and acts – even in the way he treats me."

The chief waited. "Go on."

"Hal wouldn't even lie to me the other night so's he could go to that scavenger hunt." Big Ed shook his head vigorously. "No sir, if Hal told you he didn't have nothin' to do with that drugstore robbery, then he didn't."

"Ed, you know that most parents don't like to admit that their own children can get into trouble."

Big Ed Seybold shook his head. "What do I have to do to make you understand? I'm not sayin' Hal didn't break into that drugstore because he's a kid of mine." His lips curled in bitterness and self-reproach. "I'm sayin' he didn't break into that drugstore because– because he's a Christian. He doesn't lie. He doesn't cheat at school, and he's nice to me when I'm so mad at everyone that I try my best to get him to spout off at me so's I can cuss him out."

The chief was impressed. "I want you and Hal both to know that we don't want to cause trouble for either Hal or Jim Morgan. If they aren't guilty, we're going to do everything we can to uncover evidence to prove it." His face darkened. "And if they are guilty, we're going to do everything we can to get enough evidence to find them guilty." He talked with Hal for a few minutes and finally put on his coat and left.

When they were alone together once more Hal turned to his dad, tears glistening in his eyes. "Th-thanks a lot for sticking up for me."

Big Ed swallowed with great difficulty. "What kind of a man would I be if I didn't stick up for my own boy?" He went over to Hal, awkwardly, and put his arm about the boy's shoulder. "It's goin' to take a sight more than Chief Clark to make me believe you robbed anyone, Hal."

The words choked in his throat. Hal, looking up, saw a big tear trembling on his dad's eyelid. The boy smiled. The fright that had gripped his heart began to seep away.

* * *

Danny Orlis had started to take off his shoes before going to bed when there was a knock on the door and Big Ed Seybold came bursting in. His face was a hard, immobile mask and his eyes glinted.

"I want to talk to you, Orlis!" He glanced in Kay's direction. "You got any place we can talk alone?"

Kay spoke up quickly. "You can stay right here, in the living room if you like, Danny. I'm going on to bed."

Big Ed did not sit down. It was not until the door closed behind Kay that he spoke again. He stood self-consciously before Danny, twisting his cap in his hands. "I–I've got troubles, Orlis!"

"Is it something I can help you with?"

Big Ed's face darkened. "You prob'ly don't think I'm much of a dad. I guess I know my faults in that department better than anybody else," he said. "But I've been tryin' to do what's right to Hal. I've been a-tryin' to raise him up so he'll be a better guy than his old man!"

The young man nodded. "I suppose you're talking about this trouble Jim and Hal are in."

"That's right. The boys might be in trouble, but I know them kids! I know they didn't break into that drugstore!"

"You and I think alike on that, Ed."

Mr. Seybold pulled up a chair and sat down across from Danny, breathing heavily. "I don't know anything about any evidence they could have, but I know that Hal and Jim both mean business with God!" he exclaimed.

He crossed his legs and uncrossed them nervously. "The last couple of months or so it hasn't made any difference how mad I got at Hal, he never even raised his voice to me. And his grades and conduct at school are better. It just don't make sense for him to be like that around home and at school, and then go and do something like they're trying to claim that he and Jim did."

For half an hour or more the two men talked in low tones. At last Ed Seybold arose to go. His concern and nervousness seemed to have grown with the passing of time.

Danny followed him to the door. "Before you go, Ed, there's something else I'd like to talk to you about."

The big man came back, hesitantly.

"You've been telling me about the change in Hal's life, and that you realize it's genuine. Wouldn't you like to have the same thing happen in your life?"

Big Ed Seybold sat down. "It ain't for me, Orlis," he said. "I've been in the same old rut too long. God wouldn't be interested in the likes of me.

"That's not what the Bible says. The Bible says, 'The one who comes to Me I will certainly not cast out.' "

Danny continued to talk with him about his soul. Big Ed Seybold pulled his chair closer. There was a new look on his face – a look of interest and concern for his soul – a look that was much like belief.

At last, Big Ed Seybold stood to his feet. "Orlis, it ain't that I don't believe you, but I've just got to think about it. This here Christian business is all new to me. I'll think it over."

A new look of hope came across Danny's face after Big Ed left. He knew the Lord was working in Big Ed's heart, and there was now a greater desire than ever in Danny's own heart for the big miner's salvation.

CHAPTER 11

A WITNESS BEARS FRUIT

Hal waited up for his father for a while, but finally went to bed. He was asleep when Big Ed finally came home that night. The next morning when he got up and dressed, his father was already up, sitting in a chair and staring at the stove.

Big Ed Seybold lifted his gaze slowly without speaking. Hal went past him toward the kitchen, but his father stopped him. "Come back here and sit down." His voice was as gruff as it had ever been, but there was a strange quality in it – a quality Hal had never heard before. "I want to talk to you."

Hal stared at him uncertainly but did as he was told.

It was two or three minutes before Big Ed spoke again. "I went over to see Danny Orlis last night."

Hal said nothing, but his pulse quickened, and moisture came out on his forehead.

Never much for speaking, Big Ed fought the words

out, one by one. "To tell you the truth, I almost took on this Christian business you and Orlis talk about all the time." He paused. "Maybe I should have done it."

Hal stared at him. "But, Dad, you can still do it. When I became a Christian, I just told the Lord that I was a big sinner and needed Him to straighten me out."

"But you wasn't as bad a sinner as I am, boy," he said. "I'm a drunk and a cheat and a liar."

"But that doesn't matter, Dad. The Bible says that Jesus died for everybody."

"That's what Orlis said too."

"I've never been happier in my life, Dad, since I became a Christian."

"Hal, I've got to tell you something. The things Danny Orlis talked with me about really got under my skin, but I started thinking about this Christian business before last night. Why, you've been showing me that there really is something to this Christian stuff. That was the thing that got me. The more I kicked you around, the nicer you seemed to be." He took a deep breath. "That and the fact that if you hadn't been a Christian, you might really have been in on this Mason's drugstore affair. If you'd followed my example, that's just about where it would have led you."

Hal's eyes brightened and a broad smile broke across his puzzled face. "Dad!"

Big Ed returned his smile, briefly. "You don't know how I've been a-fightin' against this thing. That's why I've been givin' you such a rough time. But last night when I was talking to Orlis, I almost decided that I couldn't fight against God no more."

Hal choked and swallowed hard. "Dad, why don't you accept Christ right now? I'll get my Bible and show you some of the things that Danny showed me the day I became a Christian."

Big Ed nodded solemnly. Together he and his son knelt by a kitchen chair as Hal led his father to the Lord. After both of them had prayed, they got up from their knees. Now Hal could see a different look in his father's eyes.

"Hal, I couldn't sleep any after I got home last night. Never slept at all. I was thinkin' and thinkin' of all the things I've done and been a-doin'. Things that were downright wicked." He paused momentarily. "I'm not like you, Hal. You cleared things up before you were old enough to have had sin get a strangle hold on your life the way it's done to me. I–I've got to do a heap of changin'." He sighed deeply.

"But Dad, you won't have to do everything alone now. God promises in the Bible to help us when we call on Him – and I'll sure do everything can.

Instead of replying, Big Ed took a package of cigarettes from his pocket and looked at it intently. "Take these things. I've been usin' them since I was ten years old. I'm goin' to need a lot of help to get them out of my life."

With a sudden, impulsive gesture he ripped the cigarettes in two and threw them into the stove. "And that's not all I've got to quit doin'. I've been giving you a rugged time of it."

"It hasn't been so bad. And now that you're a Christian, all of that's over.

Big Ed shook his head. "Now, don't be too sure it's over, Hal. I know myself better than you know me. I'll be tempted to keep right on growlin' at you and tryin' to shove you around. You've got to help me with things like that. You've got to help me a lot."

Hal was beaming at him. "You'll have a lot better help than me from now on, Dad," he said. "You'll have God to help you."

That night again, Hal got his Bible and began to read from it. Then he and his father bowed their heads and prayed. Big Ed's prayer was hesitant and stumbling but sincere. Hal's heart just sang!

* * *

Danny and Kay Orlis were in the living room when they heard a heavy footstep on the porch, followed momentarily by a brisk knock. Danny opened the door to greet Chief of Police Clark who was standing there frowning.

"Good morning, Mr. Clark," Danny said, smiling. "Won't you come in?"

The big man remained in the doorway, uneasily. "I'm sorry to bother you, Orlis, but I came to get Jim Morgan. Is he here?"

Danny and Kay went down to the police station with Jim. When they got there, Ed and Hal Seybold were already there, standing together in one corner of the sparsely furnished little office.

"We brought you to the station," Chief Clark said, "to go through the necessary formalities and then release them in your custody, if you are willing to accept the responsibility and will guarantee that the boys will be in court on the day of the trial."

Danny and Big Ed spoke almost in unison. "We'll promise to have them back here any day and time that you say."

Jim and Hal stared at one another miserably. They tried to speak but could not bring themselves to do so.

The formalities at the police station only took a moment or two. And when they were over, Hal's father turned to Danny. "Looks bad, doesn't it?" he asked.

The young flier nodded in agreement. "But they're not guilty until they've been proven guilty.

Big Ed moved closer and lowered his voice. "What are we goin' to do, Orlis?"

Danny thought for a moment. "I suppose we should see a lawyer the first thing Monday morning and–"

Big Ed's face clouded. "I don't know what's the matter with these cops. They know Hal and Jim aren't the kind of boys that have been giving them trouble."

They left the police station and all went over to Danny and Kay's together.

"I don't understand why they keep talking about

the evidence they have against the boys," Kay Orlis said. "Hal was home and Jim was at the scavenger hunt all evening."

"That's what I've been a-sayin' to Chief Clark, Mrs. Orlis," Big Ed put in, "but it don't do no good." He paused significantly. "You see, I wasn't there all evening to prove that Hal was home and in bed." His lips curled bitterly. "I just had to go out and get myself a drink! If it weren't for that, I could give the boys an alibi myself!"

While the adults were talking, Hal and Jim went into the kitchen and closed the door. Hal turned to his companion. "Boy, Jim, I've never been in a mess like this before."

The Morgan boy swallowed hard.

"What are we going to do?"

Jim pushed his fingers nervously through his hair. "All we can do is nose around and try to find out who really did break into the drugstore."

There was a short silence. "Boy, that'll be tough to do. The only evidence the police have found points to you and me, like that glove of mine."

Jim's forehead crinkled. "Speaking of that glove of yours, how do you suppose it got into the drugstore?"

"The funny thing about it is that I hadn't worn those gloves for several weeks. I looked and looked, but I could only find one of them."

Jim's voice was a whisper. "Do you know what I'm thinking, Hal?" he asked. "Pete Nolan and Doug Ellis swore that they were going to get even with you."

Hal breathed very slowly, and it was some time before he continued. "Doug has always had sticky fingers – ever since I first knew him up at Tanbark."

"I didn't know that, but I figure anyone who would beat up on you the way they did would break into a drugstore if they got a good chance and thought they could get away with it."

Hal got to his feet and walked to the window and looked out in the direction of the Nolan house. "I sure would hate to accuse them if they weren't guilty."

"Just the same, I think we should talk it over with Danny. Maybe he'll have some ideas about it."

When they went back into the living room, Hal's dad had already gone back to the house.

"Danny," Jim said, "we'd like to talk to you about something."

They sat down on the sofa and told him what they had been thinking.

"I'm glad you came to me instead of telling it to everyone you meet." He paused and took a long breath. "But to tell you the truth, guys, I've been thinking the same thing myself. They have what they think are real good reasons for wanting to get you two into some bad trouble."

"What do you think we should do about it, Danny?"

He thought for a moment. "All we have is our own suspicions. We don't have any evidence to present to Mr. Clark. I'm afraid he would feel that we were trying to shift the blame to someone else in order to get you boys out of difficulty." A few moments passed. "I don't think we would want to go to the authorities anyway unless we had some good, solid evidence that Doug and Pete actually are guilty."

Hal Seybold's face fell. "I suppose you're right. It sure isn't any fun to be blamed for something you didn't do."

Jim's brow gathered and his eyes darkened thoughtfully. "I know you're right, Danny, but how are we going to find any evidence that Doug and Pete are guilty? Everything the authorities have found so far has been pointing to Hal and me.

Hal got to his feet uneasily. "And if we don't find something before long to prove that we didn't break into that drug store, it won't do us any good. They'll probably send us off to–to some kind of reformatory."

Danny broke in quickly. "Now, Hal, don't talk that way. We know you guys aren't guilty, and we're going to stand beside you and help you prove it to Mr. Clark and everyone else in town."

CHAPTER 12

THE MYSTERY IS SOLVED

Silence gripped the Orlis living room. Hal Seybold and Jim Morgan were sitting across from Danny. They glanced at one another uneasily and turned toward their host. Hal ran his fingers through his hair and wet his lips with his tongue.

"I just don't know where to begin, Danny."

"The authorities have spent their time at the drugstore. If I were you guys, I'd go out and nose around the place where Pete and Doug hang out. You just might find something that would tie them into it."

Jim Morgan got to his feet and reached for his cap. "I suppose it's worth a try, anyway."

Hal and Jim left the house and crossed the vacant lot toward the place where Pete and Vic Nolan lived.

"Any ideas about where to start?"

The Morgan boy shook his head. "Nope." "I suppose

we could go over to Pete's place. They've always been around his barn a lot, but if they're home–"

"Don't look now," Jim whispered, "but there they go now, off toward town."

Hal cast a quick glance in the direction Jim had pointed. They slowed their pace until the Nolan boys and Doug Ellis were out of sight.

"I still don't have any idea of what we're looking for, Hal."

The Seybold boy frowned. "I was just thinking, Mr. Mason always kept the money in a canvas bag. We just might find it."

Jim shook his head. "They surely wouldn't leave anything that might be evidence lying around where someone might find it."

"Unless they thought they had it hid."

They left the street and started through the field where Pete and Doug played ball. Jim paused and looked about. "Now, if I were going to hide something like that money bag, I believe I'd hide it in a place like this. Nobody comes over here and it's grown to weeds and covered with old boards and junk. It'd be a good place to hide something."

"I think you've got an idea at that."

They separated and began to search the area very carefully, Hal taking one portion of the vacant lot and Jim the other.

"Find anything, Hal?" Jim asked at last.

The Seybold boy looked up and shook his head. "Not yet."

"I don't think we're going to find anything, either."

"Let's look for another ten minutes."

The additional ten minutes were almost over when Hal stopped suddenly. "Jim, come here a minute."

"Did you find something?"

"I don't know. I want to see what you think."

By this time Jim was at his side. Hal squatted and pointed at a short tire iron laying in the weeds. "Do you suppose this could be anything?"

Jim frowned. "I don't see how it could. Unless–"

Hal broke in quickly. "Unless it was used to jimmy open the window."

Jun's gaze met Hal's. He reached down to pick it up.

"Don't do that, Jim! If that is what was used to jimmy open the window, it might have fingerprints on it."

For a brief moment the boys stared at one another. "I don't believe Chief Clark has found the tool that was used to force the window. I heard someone talking about it the other day."

Hal looked about uneasily, as though expecting to see Doug Ellis and Pete Nolan striding toward them.

"You stay here and watch this thing, Hal. I'll get Danny on the double!" With that he went dashing across the field toward the Orlis home. Hal felt the perspiration come out on his forehead. If only the other boys didn't come around before Danny and Jim got back!

A few minutes later Danny drove up in his old car; he and Jim got out and they came running across the field toward him. Taking his handkerchief from his pocket, he used it to pick up the tire tool and carefully carried it to the car.

Hal got into the back seat. "Do you think Chief Clark will talk to you about it, Danny? Do you think he'll even listen?"

"Of course he will." Danny drove them to the police station and the three of them took the tire iron in to the chief.

Mr. Clark studied it carefully. "This tire iron could have been lying out in the field for months," he said. "You can find this sort of thing most anywhere. It doesn't mean anything."

Danny directed his attention to the tire tool once more. "That's what I thought at first, Mr. Clark," he said, "but then I examined it carefully. There isn't any rust on it. That means this tire iron hasn't been out in the field for any length of time. We had a lot of snow last winter and plenty of rain this spring. If the tire iron had been out there more than a few days, it would begin to show signs of rust. And if it had been there very long, it would be covered with rust. That's the way the rest of the iron on that vacant lot is."

The chief's interest began to mount. He reached over with his pencil and turned the iron over. He got to his feet. "We'll check the tool for fingerprints, then go over to the drugstore and see for sure whether this was actually the bar that was used to force the window."

Hal and Jim eyed him with growing nervousness.

Danny and the boys finally left the police station and went slowly back to the car. Hal was biting his lower lip. "What do you think, Danny? Is Mr. Clark going to let us go?"

The youthful pilot looked down at the boy. "There's no need to be so discouraged now, Hal."

Still, concern stood full in the boy's eyes. "But what if they can't find any fingerprints on that tire iron? What if it wasn't the tool that was used to break into Mason's drugstore?"

There was a short silence. Danny smiled reassuringly. "Why don't we pray and see what happens? There's no need to expect the worst now."

They stopped before the little company house where Danny and Kay lived and got out of the car.

Kay met them as they stepped up on the porch. "Danny, Chief Clark called for you."

"That's strange. We were in his office less than twenty minutes ago. Did he say what he wanted?"

"Only that he wants you and the boys to come back to the police station as quick as you can."

At the station Chief Clark and one of his officers were standing in the office studying a report when Danny and the boys entered. The chief looked up. "Well, Orlis, I've got to hand it to you. You did come up with the tool that was used to force open that drugstore window."

"I'm very glad to hear that."

The chief pulled out his chair and sat down behind

the big desk. "Yep, there's no doubt about it. The tire iron matches the marks on the windowsill. And, what's just as important, it was loaded with fingerprints."

Hal relaxed and breathed with a rush of relief.

Chief Clark turned to him and Jim. "I called you boys down here to get your fingerprints. We'd like to see if they match the ones found on the tire iron." They both held out their hands to have their fingerprints taken.

The officer took the prints into the other room. In a moment or two he was back with a smile on his lips. "Look at this, Chief. These prints are entirely different than those we found on the tire iron."

Chief Clark's face softened. "Now, that is good news." Hal looked over at the towering officer. "Does–does that mean we're free now? That we don't have to worry about s-s-standing trial, and may be g-g-going to jail?"

"We're not the ones to give the final answer, Hal. But I can tell you this much. You don't have anything more to worry about."

Danny put his arms about the boys' shoulders. "We can thank God for that."

It was almost a minute before the chief spoke again. "I want you guys to know that I'm sorry we gave you such a difficult time, and that I'm as happy as you are to find proof that you aren't guilty."

Neither Danny nor the boys realized that Chief Clark had sent for Pete and Vic Nolan and Doug

Ellis until the officer brought them into the police station. They were still sitting there when the door opened and the officer and the boys came in.

Doug stared at Hal angrily. "What're you doing here?"

Hal colored slightly. "Hi, Doug."

The other boy's lips curled in bitterness.

"What're you tryin' to do? Ring us into that drugstore mess, too?"

Hal did not reply.

Chief Clark was the one who spoke. "I'm the one who sent for you, Doug. I wanted to talk to you."

"I don't see why."

Chief Clark picked up his pencil and toyed with it.

Pete Nolan looked at him plaintively. "We haven't done anything."

Danny Orlis stepped forward. "Excuse me, Mr. Clark, but is there any reason why we should stay?"

The chief of police went over to him. "No reason at all, Orlis." He shook hands with him warmly. "I want to thank you for the interest you took in this matter and for helping us. I'm really grateful and I know the boys are, too."

Pete and Doug listened with growing concern. Doug was still defiant. "What are they trying to do?" he demanded. "Get us mixed up in that drugstore deal?"

Pete broke in quickly. "If they are, it's not going to do them any good!" he blustered. "They can't blame us guys for something that they did."

Chief Clark directed his attention to them.

"Now, nobody is trying to blame you or anyone else for anything they haven't done."

Danny touched Hal and Jim on the arm. "Come on, guys, we'd better get on our way."

They went out into the warm afternoon sun together. Once outside Hal turned to Danny. "Do you suppose Pete, Vic, and Doug really are guilty of robbing Mason's drugstore?"

Danny looked at the ground thoughtfully. "I certainly hope not. But I can't help saying that it looks awfully bad for them."

Jim went around the car and got into the front seat. "They did act scared."

"That doesn't mean too much, Jim. Look how scared you and I were, and we weren't guilty. I tell you, it's enough to scare a guy to have the police come and get him."

Danny started the engine and backed away from the curb. "That's right, Hal. And while we can't help thinking whether or not they are guilty, we want to be sure that we don't say anything to anyone until we're positive."

Danny drove down the street and turned to stop at the curb before their home. For a brief moment no one spoke. They were out of the car before Hal spoke again. "You know, I think we should go in the house and have prayer for those guys."

Danny nodded his agreement.

* * *

Chief of Police Clark waited until the door closed behind Danny, Jim, and Hal. Then he turned back to his desk. Vic shifted uneasily from one foot to the other and looked up at his older brother and Doug. Perspiration stood out on his forehead and his small hands worked convulsively. Once or twice he opened his mouth as though to speak but did not.

Finally, Mr. Clark motioned them to chairs on the other side of his desk. "There are some things I'd like to talk with you about."

Doug's lips began to quiver slightly. "We don't mind answering your questions, Chief Clark," he said. "We haven't got anything to hide. But I sure don't see why you called us in here. We haven't done anything."

The chief's expression did not change. "Then you have nothing to be afraid of. We just want to get a few points cleared up."

Vic relaxed a little as Doug continued. "Hal Seybold and Jim Morgan don't like us. If they could do anything that would get us into trouble, they'd sure do it. Wouldn't they, Pete?"

The older Nolan boy agreed. "They sure would," he put in. "Just because we wouldn't let them into our club, they've been awful mad at us. They told us they were going to do anything they could to get even."

The chief of police picked up the tire iron and

quite deliberately turned it in his hands. "This is an interesting little item. Have you ever seen it before?"

The Ellis boy stiffened, and Pete caught his breath.

"Yes, this is a very interesting little item. In fact, we checked it and found that it definitely is the tool that was used to pry open the back window of Mason's drugstore the night it was robbed."

The boys' faces paled slightly, and Vic grasped the arms of his chair with trembling hands. Doug bristled. "What's that got to do with us, Mr. Clark? Why are you telling us about it? We—we never saw it before."

The chief continued as if Doug had talked into thin air. "We found some very good fingerprints on it, prints that must have been left there by the ones who used it."

Their eyes widened and they scooted forward in their chairs, their bodies tensing.

"You guys wouldn't object to having your fingerprints taken, would you?"

Vic gasped audibly and he glanced first at his brother and then at Doug. Doug was the one who answered. "I don't see why that is necessary. You haven't got any evidence. We—we haven't done anything."

Pete broke in quickly. "That's right. I don't know why we should let you."

The chief laid the tire iron back on the desk. "It's strange that you guys feel that way." He spoke quietly. "We asked Hal and Jim the same question, and they didn't object at all. In fact, they were glad to have us get their prints. That was the way we proved that they were telling us the truth."

Doug squirmed in his chair and the older Nolan boy began to chew on his lower lip. The chief of police noticed them both but said nothing. Instead he opened a drawer in his desk and took out an ink pad.

At the sight of it Vic rose from his chair. "You don't have to fingerprint us. We did it! Doug, Pete, and I r-r-robbed the drugstore!" He sank back into his chair and began to sob piteously.

Chief Clark looked first at Doug Ellis and Pete Nolan. "You have both heard what Vic had to say. It's true, isn't it?"

There was a brief silence. Pete barely nodded. "It–it's true. We broke into the drugstore and stole the money."

"And you planted Hal Seybold's glove in the back room of the store so he would be blamed for it."

Pete looked up. "Th-th-that was Doug's idea."

Chief Clark called for a secretary to take down the boys' stories. Then he turned to the officer in the room and asked him to call the boys' parents.

Only then did Doug weaken. "D-d-do you have to tell our p-p-parents?"

Chief Clark looked up at him and spoke gently. "It's no easier for us than it is for you, Doug. But we have to tell them exactly what you have told us.

Tears came to the boy's eyes. "It–it'll break Mom's heart if you do."

Chief Clark took a long while in answering. "That, Doug, is something you should have thought about before you got into this mess. It's the natural result of getting into trouble with the law."

* * *

That night Big Ed Seybold and Hal went over to the Orlis home for dinner, as they often did recently. The big man was smiling broadly. "I've sure got to hand it to you, Orlis. I knew all along that Hal wasn't guilty, but I was beginning to think that we were never going to be able to prove it."

Danny smiled. "I hardly did anything. Actually Hal and Jim cleared themselves. They went over to the vacant lot near the Nolan boys' home and found the tire iron. All I did was to go over and look at it and get in touch with Chief Clark."

Big Ed crossed his legs and leaned back in the chair comfortably. "I feel sorry for those boys and their parents."

"So do I," Danny answered, "but I'm glad they were caught. It will be better for them in the long run. They've learned they can't get away with things like that."

Big Ed took a deep breath. "I guess I have you to thank for a lot of things, Danny. If it hadn't been for you talking to Hal about his need for a Savior, the chances are he'd be in that mess, too."

"Don't thank me, thank the Lord."

"And," Big Ed went on, "if it hadn't been for that I'd still be lost and drinking every day." He paused momentarily. "You know, Danny, I couldn't take your preachin' at me. I couldn't take Hal's preachin'; but I was impressed by the way he was livin' there in the house. That really got hold of me."

A smile broke across his broad face. "And it's the most wonderful thing that ever happened to a guy. I can tell you that!"

www.ingramcontent.com/pod-product-compliance
Lightning Source LLC
Chambersburg PA
CBHW060505300726
48975CB00008B/2652